Surrender

by
A. R. Shaw

Copyright © 2016 A. R. Shaw
All rights reserved.

ISBN: 1534985360
ISBN 13: 9781534985360
All rights reserved. No part of this publication may be reproduced, distributed or transmitted in any form or by any means, including photocopying, recording, or other electronic or mechanical methods, without the prior written permission of the publisher, except in the case of brief quotations embodied in critical reviews and certain other noncommercial uses permitted by copyright law. For permission requests, write to the publisher, addressed "Attention: Permissions Coordinator."

Publisher's Note: This is a work of fiction. Names, characters, places, and incidents are a product of the author's imagination. Locales and public names are sometimes used for atmospheric purposes. Any resemblance to actual people, living or dead, or to businesses, companies, events, institutions, or locales is completely coincidental.

Cover Designs by The Book Designers
Edited by Create Space

*Dedicated to my friends and family,
those that put up with the hermit in their midst.*

Books by A. R. Shaw

The Graham's Resolution series
A Prequel (Coming Soon)
The China Pandemic
The Cascade Preppers
The Last Infidels
The Malefic Nation

~ ~ ~

The French Wardrobe

~ ~ ~

Surrender the Sun
Book 1

~ ~ ~

Perseid Collapse Kindle Worlds
Deception on Durham Road
Departure from Durham Road

Wayward Pines Kindle Worlds
Kate's Redemption

Bite-Sized Offerings
An Anthology Addition
Zombie Mom

Contents

Books by A. R. Shaw 3
Chapter 1 7
Chapter 2 17
Chapter 3 23
Chapter 4 29
Chapter 5 33
Chapter 6 41
Chapter 7 47
Chapter 8 49
Chapter 9 51
Chapter 10 55
Chapter 11 59
Chapter 12 71
Chapter 13 79
Chapter 14 92
Chapter 15 94
Chapter 16 96
Chapter 17 100
Chapter 18 106
Chapter 19 110
Chapter 20 114
Chapter 21 116
Chapter 22 124
Chapter 23 128
Chapter 24 132
Chapter 25 134
Chapter 26 136
Chapter 27 139
Chapter 28 143

Chapter 29	147
Chapter 30	150
Chapter 31	155
Chapter 32	157
Chapter 33	160
Chapter 34	169
Chapter 35	172
Chapter 36	178
Chapter 37	186
Chapter 38	188
Chapter 39	192
Chapter 40	194
Chapter 41	198
Chapter 42	200
Chapter 43	203
Chapter 44	205
Chapter 45	210
Chapter 46	212
Chapter 47	214
Chapter 48	220
Author's Note	221
About the Author	222

Chapter 1

October 31, 2030
Coeur d'Alene, Idaho

Lying on her blanket-strewn queen-sized bed, the one she'd once shared with Roger, Maeve dreamed. He was there again...with her, laughing as she complained about him leaving his coffee cups everywhere in the garage growing islands of fluffy green mold. "It wouldn't kill you to put them in the dishwasher yourself, you know."

Levering open the dishwasher door, she made a show of turning the dirty mug upside down and placing it on the top rack. "See, it's that easy. Even easy enough for *you* to do." He grabbed her around the waist and tickled her until she squealed.

"Easy, huh?" But the tone of his voice meant something entirely different than the ease of washing moldy mugs.

But as she glanced down, pasty blood covered his camo trousers, causing them to turn a shade of puce as the red mingled with the brown. She begged him to release her and knew the deceit of the scene then.

As he quickly lifted her up into his embrace, she stole one last look into his eyes before the dream faded and he was snatched from her again. Before he left her, she reached up and pressed her hands against his rough cheeks, engulfing him so that she would remember him this time, the feel of his pressed lips to hers. She held the illusion even as his form began to dissipate no matter how hard she willed to hang on to him. "I love you. Don't leave me."

Her hand moved over the soft, rumpled sheets then, in the space he should have been but would never be again. Burying her face into the covers, she sobbed as dawn brought yet another day with the realization she'd lost him forever.

"Mom?"

Maeve wiped away the tears before she turned to her six-year-old son standing in the doorway. "Good morning, Ben. I'll be up in just a second, buddy."

"You were dreaming again. I heard you."

Like many mornings before, she needed to divert the conversation, or they'd both end up in turmoil with past memories and ghosts haunting them throughout the day. "Hey," she said, "you have a Halloween party today, right?"

"Uh huh," he said as he padded barefoot to her bedside. She pulled him closer. Ben's little boy smell still made her ache. His features were so like Roger's, set in miniature. His dark hair and brown eyes were the color of milk chocolate. She adored that Ben resembled his father more than herself. At least she had a permanent part of her dead husband after all.

She brushed her son's overgrown bangs out of his eyes then hugged him tighter. She knew he sensed her sadness. Fending off her emotions, she needed to pull strength from somewhere else deep inside for the both of them today. This was the wrong way to start the day; she knew that by repetition.

Drawing a smile to her lips, she kissed him. "Go get your cowboy costume on and I'll get in the shower. Scoot."

"OK, can I have cereal for breakfast this morning?"

"That would be far too much sugar with class treats later today. How about some oatmeal instead?"

He nodded and then sprinted down the carpeted hallway to his bedroom as she yelled, "Walk please."

Resigned to the fact that she now had to start the day, Maeve sat up and pulled her legs over the side of the bed. Running her hands through her long red hair, she tried to pull her wild mane behind her. In doing so, she glanced at the picture on her bedside table. The image with her and Roger and the infant Ben. The proud parents that somehow made this miracle stared back out at her with perfectly drawn happiness in their expressions; not a hint of tragedy marred their faces.

The Maeve today barely recognized those people. How the pain of losing Roger hurt as if his death had happened just the day before! She resented the picture now. How could they've been so happy? Didn't they know the life they led couldn't last for very long? People died in war. Fathers, mothers, brothers, sisters, and her husband along with them. Why did they think they were immune to death? The image brought her no more joy. It only brought her jealousy now. She kept the photo there on her nightstand out of tradition, hoping that someday she'd feel something more beyond bitter resentment for having him ripped from her and her son.

Not like this. Not today.

Maeve ran her fingers through her hair again and shook them, causing her hair to wave around wildly. *Ugh, get going*, she said to herself to shed the malaise trying to possess her today. She whipped the covers to the side and moved herself to the edge of the bed. Without the warmth of the covers, she realized she could see her breath out before her in her own room. *No wonder Ben ran to his room. It's freezing in here.* She hurried to the adjoining bathroom. Starting the shower, more to warm the space than herself, Maeve removed her nightshirt and brushed her teeth as they chattered from the invading freezing temperatures.

As the room began to fog with warm steam, she stepped into the water, still clutching the toothbrush between her teeth. She would take any compromise to warm herself, and if that meant brushing in the shower, so be it.

A haze wafted up around her as she turned in the warm cascading spray and then finished the task. Once thoroughly warmed and cleaned, she dressed for the day, reluctant to leave the soothing heat of the small bathroom. Then she descended the stairs of the A-frame house and landed on the cold wood floor on the main level.

Switching on her iPad that she kept in the kitchen, she set the station to the local live news stream out of Spokane while she turned on the Keurig and began Ben's oatmeal.

"It's cold in here, Mom. I can even see my breath," Ben said as he entered the room dressed in his cowboy getup, minus the holster and six-shooters that the school frowned upon. Joining her in the kitchen, he climbed up on the barstool while watching his mom carry on with their morning routine.

"I noticed. Maybe the furnace is out," she said, and while the Keurig emitted a welcome scent, she stepped over into the hallway near the garage and checked the regulator on the wall. "I don't know.

It says sixty-seven. I can hear the furnace running. I'll push it up a little anyway. I'll have to call someone to come out and check it today."

"Look at the news, Mom," Ben said. "There's a snowstorm."

She followed his small finger pointing to the screen. The weatherman was expressing concern over the new weather disturbance coming their way. "Great, and at the end of October, too," Maeve said. She finished making her coffee while she watched the news report with her son on the iPad screen.

"KREX News reporting. Bob Madeira here. Folks, bundle up. The lowest recorded temperature in the Spokane region is seven degrees recorded back in 2002. I hate to break it to you, but it's five degrees out there right now. I'm sure there's a lot of broken pipes in the region, and area plumbers will be out in full force today. Especially for those who haven't blown out their sprinklers yet, like me...

"Residents in Coeur d'Alene are enjoying three-degree weather this morning. In fact, let's check the forecast for this week—woo wee, it's going to be a shiver-fest. The highs are well below freezing the rest of this week and into the next. Most schools have either closed for the day, or there's a two-hour late start. Check your local school. It's a deep freeze, folks, with no end in sight..."

"Fantastic!" Maeve said with a chill.

"Is it going to snow?" Ben asked with excitement. His eyes sprung wide.

"Oh...I hope not. I never thought that stuff would melt off last year. Eat your oatmeal," Maeve said and plunked his bowl down in front of him. "I'm going to start the truck and get the engine warmed up before we go."

She set her hot coffee cup down reluctantly. Maeve slid into her boots and pulled her black puffy coat on, then opened the door to the garage and felt the meaning of freezing cold hitting her face. "Three degrees, my arse...Ugh, oh." She fumbled with her zipper as her fingers became numbed. "Gosh darn it, friggin' cold out here," she grumbled on her way to the driver's side of her cream-and-black SUV, a Toyota FJ Cruiser.

Once behind the wheel, she hit the garage door opener and then put the keys in the ignition. Then the garage door made a sound unlike its usual racket. "What the heck?" she said, looking in the rearview mirror. The door remained in place.

She pressed the door opener again, and this time, it lifted maybe two inches before giving up and closing once again. "Damn thing's frozen, man…"

Maeve stepped out of the FJ. "What would Roger do?" She'd uttered this phrase countless times since his death, and it had helped her figure out how to handle many tasks in the past, though now she knew it was a reliance she needed to let go of.

She scanned his workbench, remembering him squirting something from a blue spray bottle that he kept inside the door during the coldest months of winter.

"Where is that thing?"

She rifled through a few boxes of random automotive bottles and then found the one she was looking for. Maeve unscrewed the lid and smelled the contents. "Vinegar?" After replacing the top, she shook the contents. Though she knew the concoction was a year old, she hoped the solution would still work.

She began spraying the door's seal, hoping to melt whatever was frozen. Again she tried the door after waiting a few seconds, and though the door did open, it opened a bit slower, like a cranky old man rising from his bed with enough complaints and resentment to color the rest of his day with a bad attitude.

Maeve stood there looking at the frozen landscape outside her home in amazement. She could swear the month was January instead of October: everything was covered in a determined layer of frost and appeared brittle before its time. The sugar maple in her front yard had yet to lose all of its bronzed leaves—each leaf perfectly caught in a colorful stagnation now encapsulated in white crystals. Mounds of leaves were scattered everywhere over the graveled driveway and covered with a thick layer of icy frost. The long road leading to their private twenty acres within the Coeur d'Alene National Forest was beset with wild critter trails, their footsteps marking their paths from an early emergence of the day regardless of the human interlopers.

She blew out an icy breath. "Wonderful…" Though she didn't think the conditions were really any kind of *wonderful*. She meant the statement as sarcasm—the beauty of the frozen scene was undeniably a beautiful winter scene, just far too early in autumn.

She turned on her heel and started the FJ; this time though, it took two tries to get the cold engine to comply with her request. She remembered Roger telling her once that cold weather was as hard on engines as it was on people. She doubted him then, though now it seemed his statement was redeemed.

"Ben, get your big coat on and gloves and your hat," she said as she entered the now-warmed house once again.

"Do I have to? No one else will be wearing theirs," Ben complained.

"No, you don't, but take one step out there without your warmest gear on and you'll lose your nose to frostbite. You don't really need those fingers either, do you?" She shook her head in mock agreement.

"Mom!" Ben rolled his eyes.

"Seriously, you heard the weatherman. Bundle up, buddy."

"OK," Ben said as he climbed off the stool, taking big steps with slumped shoulders up the stairs. He finished his morning routine with the reluctant addition of winter gear while Maeve finished her now lukewarm coffee, cleaned out Ben's breakfast bowl, and listened to the news while she packed their lunches and grabbed her gear for the day.

As Maeve pulled out of the long driveway and drove away from the house, she was thankful for the choppy gravel drive. She would have slid on the sloped icy frost halfway down the path without the benefit of the grit. However, once she pulled off of Scenic Bay Drive onto the nicely paved Beauty Bay Drive, she began sliding to the other side of the road. The slick street made it nearly impossible to gain traction even after she put the FJ into four-wheel drive.

"Well, that wasn't the way I'd planned it."

Chapter 2

Maeve opened the bookshop door with the force of her body and leaned hard against the glass door pane. Once inside, she was so cold that her breath was as apparent inside as out. "Don't they have the furnace on yet?" she said with no one to hear since her employees were not scheduled to arrive until later in the afternoon when business typically picked up.

She shook off her gloves and squeezed her fingers open and shut, trying to get them to work like normal.

She'd barely made it into town after dropping Ben off at Fernan Elementary School. Everyone remarked how terribly cold it was so early in October. Admonishments that the school should have called a two-hour-late session were whispered none too quietly down the hallways.

"Don't stand outside for me," she'd told her son. "Wait inside until you see me in the turnaround. OK, Ben?" She didn't want him to freeze outside after school, and sometimes the teacher's aides couldn't be trusted to take the right care in severe weather.

"Yes, Mom," he'd said, but she still doubted his words; he would be given to peer pressure and little boy attitudes by the end of the day.

Still, she stifled her motherly fears knowing he'd be fine, and while she doubted there would be much traffic today with the weather, she got the bookstore ready anyway. Perhaps a few patrons would come out just to get warm in her bookstore after watching the latest hit at the movie theater less than a block away.

Maeve opened the bookstore when Roger was deployed with some inheritance money she gained after her mother had passed away. She had hoped the work would be enough to divert her from her husband's absence. The new Stoneriver complex proved to be a great asset to Coeur d'Alene with its new theater and shops. Several restaurants occupied the once-vacant stores, and with the almost occupied condos above, they were certainly out of the financial woes that were present when the complex started back in the early 2000s.

She'd only just started making headway in the ledger books when she was notified of Roger's untimely death. Now, she hoped the shop's income would be enough to support her and Ben the rest of the way. Roger's retirement she didn't touch. Those funds went into an account exclusively for Ben to someday use as his college trust as he saw fit. At least there was that. She didn't have to worry about where the money for college would come from.

The few employees Maeve kept did inventory in the evenings and worked part-time on the weekends while the others filled in. Maeve kept herself for Ben most weekends and worked days until he was out of school. That way, he would have some semblance of a normal life. That was how she saw it in her mind anyway. A normal life for a little boy without a father. One she could never replace anyway.

After turning on the cash register computer system, Maeve checked the back door and looked for any packages left for her. She'd been expecting a shipment from Ingram Content any day, and though today would mark the shipment one day late, she wasn't worried. The ice on the roads was holding everything back; she'd already received a shipping delay notice in her e-mail.

A familiar jingle caught her attention. She returned to the front of the store, only to find Elizabeth, the lady that ran the sports store next door, standing inside.

"Maeve."

"Yes, I'm here," she said as she rounded the many shelves containing the books she loved.

"Did you hear?"

"Hear what?"

"The water pipes in my unit froze and burst. There's no water."

"No, I didn't hear. Are they coming to fix it?"

"No, not yet. All the condos above are also out of water. Isn't this something? Three degrees at the end of October? At this rate, we'll be in a deep freeze by Christmas."

"Oh gosh, don't even say that."

"Well, it's true. Didn't you hear about the preordained Ice Age? Many scientists have predicted this for a long time. It's all over

"You're a bad driver," Ben announced with confidence from the backseat.

She checked her son in the rearview mirror, arched her eyebrow, and asked, "Whoever told you that I was a *bad* driver?"

"That's what Grandpa Jack says."

Maeve let out a frustrated breath. "I am *not* a bad driver. Grandpa Jack tells that story of when I was *learning* to drive. I haven't run into a police officer since I was a teenager." She began to drive down their sparsely inhabited road as she left. "I'm going to have to have a talk with Grandpa Jack next time we go to Maine. What are you laughing about back there?"

Ben giggled again. "You," he said, pointing. "Ran into a *policeman*!"

"Agh! Some things you never live down. I swear even your…"

She swallowed hard. She'd done it again. She'd forgotten…As impossible as it was to forget her husband's death, it happened from time to time, even now. "Even your dad used to give me a hard time about that one." She ended her statement with a smile and then glanced in the rearview mirror to see how Ben had taken the mention of his father again.

She found him with a half-smile staring out the window. It wasn't *so* bad now. A month ago she couldn't even mention Roger's name without Ben and herself resorting to tears still or at least a painful knot in their throats. Now, it was just the painful knot and a clenched stomach. *Time heals all wounds? That's a trick I'd like to see*, she thought, still glancing at her boy's reflection as he appeared to brace for impact.

"Mom!" Ben shouted with his arm outstretched. With a sickening crunch, a blurry rust-brown beast flitted to the side of the road. Careening recklessly, the SUV skidded out of control, finally coming to a stop on the icy, narrow, winding two-lane street.

Her heart pounding like a racing piston, Maeve turned to her son. "Ben! Are you all right?" Her hands shook like leaves. "Ben?"

"Yes, Mom, I'm fine. You hit him, I think?"

"Was it a deer? A moose? I didn't even see what it was." She scanned the windows to catch a glimpse with hopes she hadn't killed the unknown creature.

"You hit a *man,* Mom! It was a man on a horse. It was the hermit guy, I bet."

"Oh my goodness!"

"You hit him, Mom!"

"Oh jeez," she said. There were tracks in the icy frost on the road leading off the side and into the forest, but she didn't see anyone, man or beast, out there anywhere.

Sitting sideways in the middle of the road, she restarted the SUV and then pulled the truck over to the side of the road with her emergency flashing lights on. "Stay right here, Ben," she said as she released her seatbelt that now clenched across her lap like a vise. This stretch of Beauty Bay Road traversing through the thick forest was always her favorite part. She could breathe deeply here in its seclusion and felt peace unlike anywhere else in the world. It wasn't until five more miles up the two-lane road that her breath became more shallow and tense as the small town of Coeur d'Alene came into view.

Roger often told her the thickly forested area was home to several ex-military men who just couldn't take society anymore after the trauma of war and used the forest as a sanctuary of sorts. They lived off the land there, and now Maeve was afraid she'd just killed or maimed one of them, the one they called the Hermit.

"Hello?" she shouted after she quickly shut the door to keep the warmth inside of the truck for Ben. She cupped her hands around her mouth and yelled, "I didn't mean to hurt you. Are you all right?" She waited for a response as she followed the tracks in the frost leading from the road into the evergreen forest. They became harder to detect the farther she went, as the canopy of the woods held back the frost and the evidence of footprints. Once, two feet in the dense brush, she looked back at Ben looking through the truck window after her. Her breath puffed out in little clouds in front of her face. Her nose was already numb, and her cheeks felt frozen solid. She crossed her arms and suddenly had the feeling someone was watching her, and though she was cold, there was something more making her shiver.

"I'm sorry I hit you. Please let me help," she yelled again, breaking the solitude of the forest. That's when she finally saw him and had the feeling it was only because he'd *let* her see him. A man hidden in plain sight appeared before her. Wearing military camo much like Roger's, he blended in well with the evergreen surroundings.

His raspy voice startled her. It was as if he hadn't used it in quite some time. "Don't yell. You should watch where you're going. Especially with a kid in the car," he said, motioning toward the SUV.

Her mouth agape, she finally said, "I...I'm sorry. Did I hurt you or your horse?"

"You almost did. He's fine. I think you murdered a few fallen branches on the road though. Go on. Just watch where you're going," he said gruffly, but his eyes were soft and unyielding as he held her attention.

"Can I bring you anything?" she said, assuming he was the hermit Ben mentioned.

"I have everything I need."

She took the hint that he wanted her to leave. "OK. OK then. I'm Maeve Tildon," she said and held out her hand for him to shake.

He stared at the offering.

Her hand hanging in midair for longer than a comfortable time, she let it drop. "If you find out later that you, or your horse, are hurt...well, I live down Scenic Bay Road. There's a sign on the mailbox that says Tildon. You can't miss us. Just let me know. I'll pay for any medical expenses or vet bills," she said and turned her head toward her SUV, then suddenly turned back again. "I'm just *very* sorry." As if she really wanted him to know she truly was.

He nodded at her and diverted his vision to the side.

She figured that was the end of their short conversation, and she turned to leave again.

"Hey, you're Maeve? Roger's Maeve?"

She turned. "Yeah. I mean, I...Roger...he died. Over...there."

The man stood there a moment, silent, maneuvering the news around in his head as if a puzzle piece he'd tried to fit into place had found home. She knew the feeling.

"I hadn't heard. I'm sorry. When?"

Caught off guard, she said, "Almost a year now. Did you know him?"

He took a step back. "Yeah. I knew Roger."

She responded the way she always did. With sad eyes, she smiled slightly because there was no way to respond appropriately to having someone ripped from you. If there was, she hadn't figured it out yet. She turned, and when she did, she did it into herself. Set back a mile in grief in an instant, again.

She walked back to the opening from the forest to her truck holding her son. Then she turned, and this time when she looked back, the man was gone. Vanished into the woods.

She never did see the horse she'd nearly hit.

Shaking her head as if his image had been a dream, she made her way back to the SUV and climbed inside, noticing it was nearly as cold inside now as it was outside. Ben was shivering in his car seat.

"Did you find the Hermit?"

"I found a *man*. It's not nice to call someone a hermit, Ben."

She started the truck.

"What's his name then? That's what they call him at school. He has a horse. Was the horse hurt?"

"Far too many questions all at once, son. He didn't mention his name, and it looks like they're both fine, thank goodness." She lowered the emergency brake handle and restarted the engine.

"Let's go. You're going to be late for school this morning."

the news. I remember my mother talking about it when I was a teenager. She said the same thing happened back in 1645 and the Thames in southern England froze over. They ice-skated on the river. There are old paintings about it. 'It's happened before. It'll happen again,'" she said. "Like an abusive husband." Elizabeth laughed.

"Are you going to close up shop then?" Maeve asked, thinking closing up might be a good idea for her, too.

"I have to stick around and wait for the plumber to show up. *If* he shows up. But you could go home. I doubt anyone'll venture out today anyway. The streets are terribly slick, and they've closed the theater."

"School's open, though."

"Ben went in then, did he? I heard they were going to let out early."

"Well, if that's the case, I should just call Angelina and Justin and have them stay home. I'll just pick up Ben and go home and watch movies all day. Maybe make some soup and popcorn."

"That's a splendid idea. You deserve to take some time off, Maeve."

Again Maeve half smiled and backed away. Her widowhood always came up, no matter how subtle the conversation. She backed a little more and said, "Well, call me if anything happens, then. I'll just close up the store and head back and pick up Ben on the way." Maeve flipped off the cash register and then asked, "Did they say what the high today would be?"

Her friend stepped back inside the store quickly. "I heard *this* is it. Three degrees. That's why it's such a big deal. I bet I don't get any trick-or-treaters tonight with this cold weather."

"Ugh, that's right. Halloween. I might take Ben by your place, but the roads are so slick, and if this keeps up by dark it'll be more like zero degrees. Too cold to take little ones out."

"I agree, and not safe to drive on the frozen streets. Do you have anyone nearby to walk him to?"

Maeve shook her head, "No, we're out in Beauty Bay. Might as well be the boonies. We like it that way, usually."

"You could bring him to our house. Sam's home—I'll call him to have something ready; it's on your way home anyway. Then head back. I bet Halloween will be canceled for a lot of children this year. Too bad, but it's safer that way, certainly not worth frostbite."

"Thank you. That's very sweet of you, but like you said, we'll just go straight home." Maeve could always count on her friend for quick parenting advice. "I'll lock up and go get him now."

***

A few minutes later, Maeve pulled up into the school parking lot. As she walked toward the green-painted school bell of Fernan Elementary School, she wasn't surprised to see they'd put down salt on the icy parking lot again to keep the parents from colliding into one another. She also wasn't surprised to see that several parents also had the practical idea of picking their kids up early on this treacherous weather day. The parking lot was full to overflowing. Why they didn't cancel classes in the first place confounded her.

"Hi, Maeve. Ben is in the cafeteria with the rest of the class," his teacher said as she passed by. "Did you get the text alert on your phone? Some parents are saying they didn't receive theirs."

"No, I just thought I'd close up my shop and come by early to get him because of the weather."

"That was smart of you. The furnace isn't working here, and we can't hold class in the frigid classrooms, so we alerted the call-in system, which apparently isn't working either."

"Gosh, I hope you get home early, too. It's supposed to get even colder in a few hours."

"I know. I'm worried. We live out toward the Palouse hills, and my kids have to walk quite a ways to our farm from the bus stop, and it's way too cold for exposed noses. I have to get my entire class home before I can leave and try to catch them before they start the walk home."

"I'm sorry. That's the opposite end of the lake for me, or I'd offer to help. Well, I'll get Ben out of here. I hope you get to leave earlier," Maeve said on her way to the cafeteria. She jogged a little down the hall and felt guilty, but something was telling her to hurry home. In the pit of her stomach, a funny feeling advised her to get Ben and get home *now*. Maeve rounded the corner of the cafeteria when she heard the principal, Mrs. Campbell, announce to all the children:

"Boys and girls, sometimes we have weather emergencies that might affect our plans. So I would like for each of you to please be responsible for yourselves and your younger siblings. It's simply not safe for trick-or-treating tonight, and so we are thankful that you've each been able to spend your holiday indoors with us today. When you go home, I want you all to stay safely inside. The cold temperatures are just too dangerous to be outside for any length of time. Your parents may have plans to do something else fun inside for the evening instead. In such cold weather, you could easily lose your fingers and toes, and that's not a very nice trick on Halloween. So enjoy the treats you've received here at school instead of going out this evening. Perhaps enjoy Charlie Brown on television or play family games instead. Be sure to bundle up, because no one is leaving these doors without their winter weather apparel on their person."

Maeve listened and was very thankful the school was taking the harsh weather seriously. She'd hate to think of children getting stranded off the school bus on their way home for any length of time in this dangerous cold without their coats on.

Maeve scanned the crowd for her little cowboy, and soon she spotted him with his floppy brown hat on. *It must be a parent thing. I can look into any group and zone in on my own child almost instantly.*

Ben spotted her too, and as she stood there shivering, she motioned with her hand for him to come to her. He got up from his spot on the floor and waded through the other boys and girls dressed as everything from princesses to a creative slice of pepperoni pizza.

"Hi, Mom," he said, dragging his school backpack and coat behind him.

"You ready?"

He nodded.

"You heard the principal. Put on your coat and gloves."

Ben didn't protest this time since he saw several of his buddies also putting on their outerwear. "They canceled Halloween?" Ben asked quizzically, trying to make sense of what the principal was trying to convey.

"Sort of. It's way too cold, so it's not safe to be exposed outside right now. Let's hurry and get you in the car before the parking lot turns chaotic." She took her son by his gloved hand and led him outside. One step into the frigid air and the sharp cold took their breath away. Once Ben was strapped securely in his car seat, Maeve checked the rearview mirror again. The last thing she wanted to do was disappoint her son. He'd had far too much of that already in his young six years. And a parking lot crash wasn't a good idea either since she'd had a bad driver reputation to overcome since that morning.

His unruly brown mop was turned sideways as he contemplated the issues outside of the window. "Mom? If we don't do Halloween tonight, can we do it when the temperature gets warmer again?"

With an inner sigh of relief, she smiled. "Yes, of course, Ben. I'm certain a lot of other parents are considering the same thing. Sometimes Mother Nature makes you change even the best-laid plans. We'll cuddle up by the fire tonight and eat popcorn and watch movies. Does that sound like a good idea?"

"That's a very good idea, Mom," Ben said.

Chapter 3

Though Maeve slid on the ice in the shadows of the large pine trees along the way, the trip home was uneventful, and she gave the stranger credit for it because she'd heeded his advice. The man had been on her mind all day. She knew just about everyone that her Roger had known, and not once had she ever run across this particular man with the deep-set blue eyes. She would have remembered those eyes, so piercingly blue you couldn't help but compare their vibrancy to every shade in nature.

No, she doubted she'd ever met him before, but he knew her by name. Meaning Roger had to have mentioned her to him over time. Roger did say a few of the fellas that came back with him after their third tour were too lost to serve again. He'd stated that they simply slipped into the forest and were rarely seen. She thought it must be a temporary situation, them just needing some time to adjust to life again. Others in town picked up the story. Maeve believed it was only a small-town rumor, but now she began to consider what fact might lie in those tales. Perhaps some who returned were too far gone from society to fully return. No one could blame them. Roger, when home on leave, suffered from nightmares. Even when he was still home with them, she'd lost a part of him to war even then.

Like most evenings when she returned home, she changed into her black leggings, wool socks, and Roger's denim button-up chambray work shirt that hung nearly to her knees. She'd worn the shirt more than Roger ever had, but the soft shirt reminded her of him, and she imagined she could still smell his scent between the fibers.

"Come on, Mom!" Ben called from the living room.

"Patience, son." Maeve shuffled the pot filled with kernels over the gas burner. Of course she could have just microwaved the fluffy stuff, but the kernels never turned out as good. She preferred the old-fashioned method. So with one hand held tightly over the lid, she moved the pot lightly over the gas burner to keep the corn kernels from burning as they heated and began to pop. As the sound of the grains rattling around the bottom of the pan lessened, she held the pot higher over the burner. Then, she quickly poured the contents into a large bowl and poured melted butter and kosher salt over the kernels, tossing the popped corn as she went; each bite held the perfect amount of each ingredient to perfection. "I'm almost done."

"Smells so good!"

She held the large round popcorn bowl with one arm and grabbed napkins with the other, and as the fireplace sparked and crackled, she cuddled up under a plaid fleece blanket with her son; between them, the popcorn bowl rested.

Ben looked as if he were in nirvana when she placed the bowl down in front of him. Together they watched the latest movie hit rated PG, but even so, Maeve kept the remote close at hand in case anything inappropriate showed up. She'd learned as a parent how to easily pretend to "accidentally" change the channel whenever something too risqué happened to be shown. So far Ben had not caught on, or so she hoped.

As evening began to set in as early as four, she remembered she needed to set food out for the stray cat Ben had named Jet, who often slept underneath their back porch. "I'm going to feed the cat before it gets too dark. I'll be right back." So as Ben watched the dinosaurs lamenting the newest villain in their midst, Maeve tiptoed into the kitchen to pour kibble into a bowl. When she opened the door, an intense cold blast stunned her in place. Closing the door behind her, she flipped on the back porch light. Then, in slippers, she made her way down the wooden porch steps. So cold was she, just in the chambray shirt, that she clutched her free arm around her middle and began to shiver right away.

"Jet," she called out, knowing she sounded silly—*As if the cat knows his name*—but that was the routine she and Ben had begun. The cat usually came running out of the brush but always held back a distance. It seemed he was a reluctant domesticate. Actually, the man she met today reminded her of the tomcat. Somewhere between the wild and what should be. Never to be fully tamed again and always a little broken, or so that was how they preferred life to be, him and the cat. Never committing fully to the assimilation of man or beast, but somewhere in the in-between.

Those like them were never accepted fully in any part of life. So they remained on their own and preferred it that way.

"Jet! Come on, it's too darn cold out here! Brrr," she shivered.

But Jet never emerged from the woods as he always did. She was reluctant to leave food out near the house to entice other creatures of the forest, some of which could be dangerous, but she made an exception on this cold night. "Well, I'm going to leave your bowl here," she said, and in case the cat watched her from behind the trees, he would know where she placed his dinner.

Maeve tiptoed back inside and locked the door. Then she hurried back to the warmth on the couch with her son and the fireplace.

"You're freezing, Mom," Ben complained as she slid in next to him under the covers on the warm couch.

"I know. It's freezing out there for this time of year. After the movie, we should watch the weather report again and find out what's going on before we go to bed."

As soon as the film was through, though, Ben lay asleep leaning against her side. She changed the channel and turned the volume down.

Bob Madeira appeared again on the news channel, and she'd never seen the charming meteorologist look so troubled.

"I don't see an end to this, folks. Nothing in the forecast would indicate a lessening of the current trend. It's winter no matter the calendar date. Expect snow in the morning up to eight inches in the Coeur d'Alene area. Keep your pets inside and make sure your children are bundled up if they go outside. Please limit their time to ten minutes. It's that cold. Schools are closed across the region, and please stay home if you don't have to go to work. Check in with elderly residents and make sure they have sufficient heat. Be careful out there, folks."

"Snow? Eight inches? Great."

Maeve lifted Ben up, and at six years old he was becoming too big for her to carry him for much longer. She was five foot five and hefted books all day long, but she conceded now to herself that the days were numbered when it came to lugging her son's weight around.

It was a sad realization. Had his dad been alive, he would have had a few more years of a parent carrying him around on occasion.

She climbed the stairs and placed him gently in his bed but didn't close the door so that the heat could continue to penetrate the cold, empty space. She tucked him in and then went to the hall closet to retrieve another blanket to spread out across him. "Good night, Ben. Sweet dreams," she whispered.

Maeve padded back downstairs into the living room and added another log to the woodstove, poking the inferno around a little with the pointy end of an iron poker that she kept nearby. The cord of wood Roger had chopped the last time he was home was quickly dwindling away, and she'd have to order some more or split some herself to keep them warm through the winter because the furnace just wasn't keeping up with the low temperatures. Their property backed up into the Coeur d'Alene National Forest, so there was plenty of downed wood to choose from. She'd have to go and see if she could round up a few smaller logs as a last resort.

Looking into the flames, she sighed deeply, trying to keep her sadness over Roger at bay. It was a daily battle. She knew it did her and Ben no good to keep mourning him. His death had been nearly a year ago now, and she wasn't crying herself to sleep at night anymore. She knew if she kept going down that long, dark, fruitless road, not only would she lose herself, but her son as well. She could not forsake Ben.

Maeve had muted the television, but she caught a glimpse of the school closures streaming at the bottom of the screen, and there flashed all of Coeur d'Alene's school districts reporting closures for the rest of the week. "That does it," she said to herself, picking herself up off the floor and retrieving a wine glass from the cupboard and a bottle of her favorite Smoking Loon Merlot. After she had armed herself with a corkscrew, she brought the items back into the living room and sipped a glass while picking at the remaining popcorn kernels that were stuck to the bottom of the wide plastic bowl while she gazed into the flames of the fireplace. That evening was the first time she'd had a drink and not sunk into the abyss of missing Roger.

Of course she missed him, but she'd crossed that bridge, and now she could enjoy the taste and honor his memory as well.

Then, suddenly, she heard a cat screech, and she nearly spilled the wine when she jumped up from the couch. "What the heck?" she said and set the glass on the end table before going out to investigate.

Remembering the intense cold, she wrapped the blanket around her shoulders before she opened the back door. Something had tripped the motion detector light Roger had installed, and Maeve believed the perpetrator was nothing more than Jet, the cat.

The door handle was icy to the touch, and when she unlocked it, the door nearly flung open by itself from the wind pressure. In only a few hours the wind had picked up and was now gusting violently. She noticed debris strewn all over the yard where earlier there were only the expected leaves of fall.

"Jet?" she called to the cat, her voice lost to the wind. She wasn't opposed to letting the cat hang out in the garage if he would only trust her enough to let him inside. "Jet, come here," she called out. Again and again, her voice was stolen by the howling wintry wind.

She stepped outside a few more feet and closed the door behind her. The light beam played with shadows on the ground, and though she saw it with her own eyes, she was confused at the same time. Where she'd loaded some of the last few logs left over from Roger's cordage, a large stack of freshly hewn logs lay. Something was out there—or rather someone—and had given her fresh wood. No human should be exposed to this weather, especially at night. She thought to herself, *What in the world?*

Maeve stepped back inside the house briefly and donned a proper jacket and insulated rubber boots. She grabbed a flashlight and gloves as well and went outside to the woodpile and shined the light beam on the ground to see if there was any sign of the mysterious wood delivery guy.

She, in fact, saw several boot prints on the frost-covered ground and followed them to the tree line where she also found hoofprints. They were fresh prints, even on the frozen ground. Then suddenly she realized who he must be and that he could still be there somewhere in the dark. The funny thing was, she wasn't as afraid of him as she thought she should be.

She cupped her hands around her mouth and let her voice carry on the wind as her wild red hair blew around her. "Thank you!"

Part of her wanted to add *you didn't need to do that*, but hadn't she just lamented about how in the world she was going to get more wood? Her home butted up against the section of the dense forest he must have come from. Maeve grabbed as much of the wood as she could carry to haul back inside with her, and when she arrived back at the porch, she saw then what she hadn't before. A neatly stacked set of wood remained beside the doorway.

"That's why Jet shrieked. That guy must have scared him." Maeve looked around once more and realized now there were snowflakes drifting on the wind. The storm was starting, and she hoped she had prepared enough for herself and Ben because it looked as if they were going nowhere for several days.

Chapter 4

Bishop kept his distance. He hadn't meant to startle the cat. In fact, he hadn't noticed the feline there in the shadows of the porch to begin with. In the past, he had always kept watch over Roger's home from a distance when he knew Roger was deployed, but he hadn't heard of his death. He assumed he'd returned and was directly deployed once more.

The dwindling force of the active components of the US military caused those who remained to pick up the slack. This meant there was very little time at home in between deployment cycles. Roger had been a damn fine soldier and friend, and Bishop felt obligated to see to it that his home was kept safe in his absence. The news of Roger's death hit him hard, and to know that his wife and kid were suffering without him really hit home. Especially since he knew there was no other family in the area to help them. Roger's family had passed away a long time ago, and he believed the wife had family back East. That was why Roger had asked him to keep an eye on them in the first place.

Especially now with the coming cold, he knew they'd need more help in the future. If his hunch were correct, they were in for more than just a little cold spell. This was foreseen. Though he and others had prepared, the coming challenge would test even the most primed among them.

He started with an assessment of the outside of Maeve's home. Not nearly enough firewood was the first thing he'd noticed earlier in the day. The second was the lack of security of the home. Anyone in need could easily trespass through the woods and take what he wanted.

The Tildons' home security was based on what was required for a polite and civil society. *That*, Bishop knew all too well, was no guarantee—not anymore. Combine the downward spiral the world seemed to be descending into with the extreme weather phenomena that some felt creeping in on them each day, and it was easy for anyone with his eyes open to fear what may come when the comfort of the civilized world was no more.

Bishop imagined that one forceful push on the back door of Maeve's home and intruders would quickly gain entry into her house. Nothing but a thin piece of flimsy wood to hold the bolt of the door's lock in place kept them at bay. No, he'd have to somehow convince her to take extra measures to ensure the home's security. Hopefully he could convey those needs without her asking too many questions. Questions required answers, and answers required talking. Talking to people was something he simply wasn't fond of anymore.

He needed to get her and the boy in safely prepared conditions before their situation became desperate. He owed that to Roger. He'd watch out for them in hopes that this early onset of winter was not what he feared it would be.

He expected the prediction of the Maunder Minimum pattern, which was caused by the lack of solar flares, would all blow over and not reach the extent that he feared, but something nagging him told him this storm was the beginning of something that would change them all.

Before the war, he'd studied the theory of the Maunder Minimum. Many scientists discounted the theory, saying the ideas were unrealistic ones, but now he doubted that logic. The same lack of solar flare patterns happened back in 1645 and lasted until 1715. This was a time before today's living standards, and many died. They'd called those thirty years the *mini ice age*. And it was happening again, now.

He'd returned to the Tildon place with split wood that evening, and while she checked out the back of the house in search of the cat, he was in the front of the property checking out the SUV's tires. He'd noticed they were leaning into the critical low-tread zone. Driving around on the icy streets of Coeur d'Alene could get her and the boy in trouble, especially the way she was driving today. With the weather this bad, she should have snow tires on already. There was no way for him to replace the tires for her, but he could make sure she didn't drive around on them tomorrow.

By today's standards, the Toyota FJ was an antique, even though this one appeared to be a 2013 model. National Automobile (NA) didn't make them. Therefore, they weren't legal to purchase anymore and their parts were scarce, especially with the new ever-increasing emissions criteria. The fact that she left the FJ there in the driveway, insecure to theft, proved to him that she was focused on her and the boy's safety above all else. These things were gold mines for the underground scrap trade. And if anyone decided to relieve her of the truck, she'd be out of a transportation unit for her and the boy. That wasn't smart, not out in the dark forest in the middle of a winter that came early in fall.

"Serves her right," Bishop said under his breath, popping the hood silently. He pulled the starter fuse from the engine and put the small component into his shirt pocket. He relatched the hood with a quick pop.

If she ever found out he was the reason her car wouldn't start, she might get angry, but keeping her and the boy inside the home where he could protect them was in their best interest—for now.

With his goal accomplished, he peeked around the corner and watched as she tracked his steps into the woods and called out to him. "You're welcome," he said under his breath and then waited for her to go back inside. He listened for her to lock the door, which she did, but there was no deadbolt, and that had to change, too.

Chapter 5

The next morning, Maeve woke from the living room couch. At first, she didn't know where exactly she was and then remembered the glass—*or was it two?*—of wine she'd had the night before. Though she enjoyed the evening at the time, she was regretting it now. Her temple throbbed a little, and she contemplated taking a painkiller but knew if she didn't eat something first she'd regret that, too.

The pain in her head and the cold had awakened her. The fire had died down, and she was freezing with only one blanket to keep her warm. Wrapping the blanket around herself, she rose from the couch and knelt once again at the fireplace. She held her hand above the coals and felt no residual heat whatsoever; only a cold draft blew over the ashes. So she made the fire all over again and soon she heard Ben descending the stairs.

"It's freezing in here," he said, stating the obvious. Ben jumped up and down while looking out of the frosted window where it was even colder, the sky slung low with a gray blanket. "It snowed! A lot! Can I go sledding after school?"

His little voice was too loud for her head so early on a slightly hungover morning. "No. I mean, there's no school today." She held her temple and closed her eyes at the thrumming.

"All right! Snow day!" Ben gladly yelled.

"Ugh, keep it down, buddy," she said, since the rise in volume made it feel like her brain would shatter all over the living room, and she didn't want that to happen in front of Ben; he'd been through enough. Then suddenly she remembered the cat last night and the stacked wood she discovered. *Was it a dream?*

She got up and went over to the dining room window where Ben stood and peered out toward the shed, and there was the wood. The pale yellow of freshly chopped wood peeked out from the layer of snow at her.

They'd have only enough firewood for the next few days if the weather kept up this cold. Otherwise, she'd still need to call someone today to bring her more.

"I'm starving, Mom. What's for breakfast?" Ben asked and climbed up on his stool at the kitchen counter.

"Ya know, if you let me shower and have a cup of coffee first, I'll make you pancakes and bacon."

"Bacon! Sure."

"Um…OK, you can watch TV while I get going," she said, with the blanket still wrapped around herself. She fixed up a cup of strong coffee, taking the steaming cup with her as she shuffled into her bedroom.

At her dresser, Maeve caught herself glancing at Roger's image in the photograph on her nightstand like she'd done every waking morning since his death. *Why must I torture myself missing him every day?* she asked herself, then felt ashamed for *trying* to move on. There was no winning in a life of mourning someone you loved and lost. No amount of growth is celebrated or achieved. There's guilt even in the minuscule milestones of healing over a loved one's death—an ever-aching guilt that only minutely alleviates over a length of time out of sheer boredom of the sorrow one feels.

She shook her head at her own folly. If she could at least stop glancing at the photo every day, she'd mark that as finally moving on. Maybe someday she could place the photo somewhere else? Perhaps on the top of the dresser, and then slowly move the reminder of Roger into the living room—maybe her room could become her own haven once again instead of the one she still shared with Roger even now.

Taking a deep breath, Maeve selected the undergarments she'd wear that day, going for the cotton ones because they were warmer than the nylon. And instead of choosing an outfit from her closet, she grabbed a white ribbed cotton tank top and a long-sleeved cotton T-shirt paired with flannel-lined black cotton leggings and the warmest wool socks she could find. This was a day for comfort, and she was going to make sure she was at least cozy, especially if she had to conserve wood.

Before she could start her shower, though, Ben came tearing into her room shouting, "Mommy, Mom!"

"What, Ben? Please don't yell. I have a headache." She bent down to his level, taking her blanket with her.

"On the TV there's a *weather alert*," he said carefully.

She stood. "OK, let's see it."

He took her hand and skipped into the living room, trying to drag her with him. "The cold weather is making you energetic, I see," she said gruffly, but she had to smile at his enthusiasm. Once she was in front of the TV over the fireplace, Maeve saw the banner reading Weather Alert in bright letters that couldn't be missed.

"Expect subzero temperatures tonight and into the coming week," Bob Madeira said looking even more graver than the night before. *"We're still technically in autumn, folks, but this isn't something to ignore. All area schools are closed, as well as work canceled for nonessential staff. Please stay home, people. Use what you have in the pantry for the coming days. If you lose power, and many of you will, use your backup supplies and check on your neighbors. If needed, go to a shelter to stay warm. If in doubt, don't hesitate."*

Maeve dropped her blanket suddenly and went into the kitchen to check the pantry and fridge. At least a week had passed without her visiting the grocery store. She usually bought food one week at a time, and she knew she was down to the last few days of her weekly menu.

First she scanned the pantry shelves, noting a few jars of spaghetti sauce and pasta, a box of taco shells, a few cans of soup, and a bag each of rice, flour, and sugar. She rifled further and found a bag of hidden gummy bears among the spices, and she tossed them on the counter. Then she checked the fridge, she pulled out the half carton of milk, which on further inspection smelled like something other than milk, and she wasn't going to take a swig to check. There were a few long-gone leftovers from past meals just taking up space; they were past their prime and needed to be thrown out. Then there were condiments galore, and after she had looked further past the dried-up parsley, several eggs, and few rubbery carrots, there wasn't much else edible in the fridge. Years ago, Roger had warned her to stock food for emergencies since they lived far from a grocery store, but she was a business owner and had little time for anything beyond her weekly grocery list, which she used an app for on her iPad to save time and money.

"We'll have to run to the grocery store after I get out of the shower."

Ben looked up at her with concerned eyes. "But the Bob Madeira guy said to stay home," he said, pointing at the TV.

"Yes, he did, but he meant that you should have your supplies *first* and then *stay home*."

"Oh, it sounded like he said not to go *anywhere*."

"Well, that's true, but we need to get a few things if we're going to be stuck here for more than three days."

Her son seemed to accept this and then asked, "Can I have some of those gummy bears?"

Maeve smiled at her son, his concern for their safety forgotten already. She patted his head and said, "Sure, why don't you get ready, too? We'll pick up breakfast in town instead of making pancakes and get our supplies early before everyone else thinks of the same thing. Then we'll come home, and I still need to call for a wood delivery," she reminded herself.

Grabbing her phone, she quickly checked Craigslist for the firewood listings she'd seen there many times in the past. When she found a listing, she called but only received a recorded message saying they were no longer delivering wood for the time being, and they had no date given for resupply or a waiting list to enter.

"Great," she said and dropped her phone on the side table and again headed for the sanctuary of her shower.

Once she stepped out of her room dressed and readied for the day, her son Ben sat on the couch waiting for her. Cuddled up under the blanket she dropped earlier but still shivering, he chewed on another gummy bear.

"Still cold in here isn't it?"

He nodded.

About to toss another log on the fire, Maeve remembered the low supply. Since they were leaving the house for a bit, she opted to save the wood until she was sure to secure more.

"OK, let's go, buddy. Get your snow boots and coat on," she said as she pulled on her gloves and donned her own hunter-green quilted jacket that contrasted with her fiery red hair. She stepped into her snow boots by the door and then knelt down to zip Ben's coat and make him pull his knit hat down over his ears. After his mittens were on as well, Maeve grabbed her purse, phone, and keys, and they headed out to the SUV in the driveway.

After they had broken their way through the eight inches of snow, she buckled Ben into the backseat and noticed how frigid the air was. His teeth already chattered with the cold. She smiled at him. Strands of her red hair flew in front of her face with a frigid gust of wind. Ben pointed behind her at something he was watching.

She turned to him as he said, "The trees...they're moving a lot."

She watched as the tops of the tall pines behind her house swayed in the harsh, cold wind. Another gust blew past her, stinging her skin. She quickly closed the backseat door to protect Ben and then seated herself in the driver's seat.

"The trees *are* moving a lot. I hope this winter storm doesn't make them come down. That's the last thing we need, unless of course it came down magically prechopped and seasoned like the load that appeared last night," she said, imagining her lack of firewood would suddenly appear from her own backyard.

"Where did that wood come from, Mom?"

Maeve put on her seatbelt and then inserted the key into the ignition. "I'm not totally sure," she said. Then she realized the engine didn't turn over. "What now?" she said and tried the key again. Nothing happened.

"What's wrong, Mom?"

"The engine's not turning over," she said, confused. She looked around, making sure everything was as it should be, and tried once more, and again nothing happened. "I don't get it. The battery isn't dead. All of the dash lights work. It's just...it's just not starting. That's just great!" she said and put her hands over her mouth to keep herself calm. *Why is this happening?*

"Did the engine freeze?" Ben asked through chattering teeth, trying to come up with a solution.

She smiled. "I don't know, son, but it doesn't look like we're going anywhere this morning. We'll have to make do with what supplies we have." She stared out of the car window at the gray sky and snow as the flakes began to blow along with the gusts, and Maeve knew she needed to get Ben inside. *This is only going to get worse.*

"Ben, go ahead and quickly undo your seatbelt and climb up here. We'll go through my door and run inside quickly."

"OK, Mom," he said, always up for the unconventional.

She quickly opened the door once Ben climbed into the front seat and then swiftly pulled him out, and they ran inside the house with the bitter wind chasing them along the way.

***

Once inside, Maeve tossed another log onto the fire first thing, poking it into place with her iron poker. As the hot embers danced in the warm, rising air disappearing up the chimney, she thought about what things she should take care of if the storm were to take the power out as the weatherman had warned earlier.

"Ben, you sleep with me for the next few nights so we don't have to heat your room. Go ahead and pick a few toys out of there, grab your pillow and blanket, and put them in my room."

"Why, Mom?" he asked, suddenly concerned.

She didn't like the look of worry on his little face and smiled. "We just need to conserve our firewood until the storm passes, so we'll close all the unnecessary doors like the hall bathroom and your room as well as the laundry room and only use the bathroom in my room and this main room. That makes sense, right?"

He nodded.

She knew letting him contribute to making some of the decisions made him feel more secure, and she'd have to keep that in mind. "I'm going to plug in all of my electronics like my computer and phone and iPad to charge their batteries. Do you have anything you want to charge in case we lose power?"

"Yeah," he said and ran off to his room.

She assumed he was gathering all of his handheld games in a hurry and various charging units to plug them in as she was doing.

Once that was done, and after she'd closed all the unnecessary doors in the house, she called her car service and explained to them that her battery must be defective or something. Unfortunately, they had no service for her area due to the storm at the time and advised her to call them back in a few days after the storm passed.

Frustrated with the call, she turned her attention to the pantry and kitchen again, feeling foolish for not preparing ahead to stay home longer than a few days with foul weather.

She tossed everything that wasn't edible and took stock of her supplies more thoroughly than before. If they ate spaghetti twice and had soup for lunch, she still had rice and baking supplies to use at her whim. She wiped the back of her hand across her forehead and wondered what culinary masterpiece she could create with rice and a few condiments. *At least I can make bread*, she thought and again thanked her deceased mother for having the forethought to teach her a few simple recipes that she always held dear. For now, she'd promised to make pancakes for Ben, and she used one of the two eggs left in the fridge to whip the dough up quickly. A roaring of rushing wind shook the house as she was about to pour the batter into the hot skillet. Ben looked at her from the living room sofa.

"Are the trees going to crash on the house?" he asked after the rushing sound subsided.

"I think it will take more than that to knock these big trees down, but a few may fall anyway. That's how nature is. The weaker ones fall so that they can make room for new growth."

She poked the bacon strips around in another skillet, noting that it was the only protein they had in the house besides half a jar of peanut butter. She would save some of the bacon just in case they needed to stretch it out, and she wouldn't give up the bacon fat either.

Once breakfast was made, she called Ben to the table and poured warmed maple syrup over his pancakes. He eagerly dug in.

Maeve also ate a pancake, and they each had two slices of bacon. After breakfast, she packed up the leftover pancakes and saved them in the fridge along with the extra bacon. She usually threw out the bacon grease, but this time she kept every bit of it in a bowl. She wasn't sure why. Her grandmother used to save bacon grease, but Maeve had never used it for anything before. She figured if her grandmother kept it she probably used it to cook with, and since Maeve had few supplies, she was saving everything possible.

After breakfast was put away and the dishes were done, Maeve scoured the house for candles, matches, flashlights, and anything else she could find or thought she might need if the power went out. In all, she had three decorative pillar candles and few books of matches from various hotels from years past as well as a butane torch lighter she used for the fireplace that was nearly empty. She also found a flashlight under the kitchen sink and another one in the garage. She wasn't sure how old the batteries were—that was something Roger always took care of. She hadn't gotten around to being the man of the house yet. Every time Maeve went into the garage, Roger's scent that permeated everything within would send her into a three-day grieving spell. As a result, she avoided the garage as much as possible.

While Ben made car noises with his handheld game, she stood back and tried to assess how many hours of candlelight they had. "Probably a couple of days if we only use them at night," she said to herself.

"What, Mom?" Ben asked.

"The candles. We have enough for probably a few days, and we have about three or four days of food hopefully..." she trailed off.

"Do you think that's enough till the storm passes and we can go to the grocery store?"

"Sure," she said, being optimistic for his sake.

"First, we have to wait for someone to come and fix our battery, and then we will go to the grocery store."

That's when the next gust of wind rattled the house. So strong was the force, that like a child playing with a toy town, it also took down several trees and power lines and, along with them, the joyful tune coming from Ben's racing game.

Chapter 6

Deep in the Kootenai National Forest, a few residents lived isolated lives among the tall cypresses, winding streams, and wildlife that roamed among them. They were part of their surroundings, unlike those men who lived on paved streets. They knew of one another and also knew where each of their neighbors resided, tucked away in hidden coves among large boulders the glaciers abandoned years past or near veiled alcoves. There were at least five hundred acres between each of them. A few of them visited one another when the need arose, to either trade something or when they had a task for more than one man, but mostly they remained alone, and those that required the isolation were left alone out of respect.

Mark Bishop was one of those men. He'd never imagined his life taking this turn. He'd started out in a pretty standard household: one mom, one dad, and a sister, growing up in a little town named Post Falls, Idaho, not far away from his current residence.

After graduating high school in 2014, Bishop headed to the University of Washington and spent four years in the rain and muck of Seattle. Then he graduated in 2018 with a shiny new bachelor's degree in atmospheric sciences and promptly fled the wet area before the ever-present mold could form on his certificate.

He'd applied for jobs a few months before graduation and instead landed a great internship with the National Oceanic Atmospheric Administration (NOAA) in Maryland for a congressional communications position. The position entailed studying oceanic and atmospheric research and giving reports to Congress. But that's as far as he got into a routine life Prewar. Things were changing.

In the spring of 2018, China attacked Japan over the disputed Senkaku Islands. An all-out war converged in the East China Sea by air, land, and water. At the time before the attack, the number of active duty members of the US military was at an all-time low since the Cold War. When the US joined the fight to protect Japan's interests, the draft was implemented immediately to bolster its numbers when the military troop casualty rate suddenly skyrocketed. The country needed more able-bodied men, and Bishop was one of them.

Bishop was drafted immediately, as his age and fitness score made him a perfect candidate. Instead of heading off to Maryland for the internship, he was measured for a head-to-toe individual protection combat uniform, taught how to use an M4, and deployed to Kadena Air Base in Okinawa, Japan. This sudden change in his life happened so quickly that he found himself shooting at the enemy only after bullets whizzed by his head as he wondered how in the world he'd arrived there in the first place or how he'd ever survive.

In the end, the task was simple: kill or be killed. That's what it all boiled down to. Gun down, bomb, or massacre as many of the enemy as possible before they killed you and your buddies. He found he was pretty good at the killing part with his M16. Because of that, and his degree, he ended up progressing through the ranks rather quickly and soon found himself directing, coordinating, and planning attacks.

That's where he met Roger Tildon. They were both part of the same unit and fought together many times. Both of them saved the other's life too many times to count. Four years of battle turned into six and then eight, and Bishop was up for recommission one day when he walked into his major's office on orders.

Standing in front of a man with gold oak leaves on his fatigues, Bishop waited in the sparse room as the senior officer typed away on the rugged laptop before him on the metal desk like some secretary at the IRS during the last day of an audit. Bishop was finally left at ease and asked to sit on a nearby hard metal chair. Bishop thought the furniture of the room was from some other era, possibly the fifties. Nothing had changed in decades.

Finally, the major stopped typing and looked up from his computer screen. Like the room, the officer himself looked like he belonged to another decade altogether. His jet-black hair with gray highlights was slicked back and plastered to his head and was flanked by silver-framed glasses and matching silver eyes. "It says here you're ready to recommission."

Bishop didn't respond because there was no question to the statement.

"You have a choice, you know? I've looked at your record, and you've served your time here, Captain Bishop. You've done your part. We're winning the battle and hope this will all be over soon. You can go home. We're starting troop withdrawal anyway."

Home? Some part of him remembered the concept, but with bullets tearing soldiers down next to you, you quickly forget what home is all about. Instead, you focused on the survival stuff. *Home* was something that could always wait.

The major continued to scan through Bishop's long list of achievements. In times past when he was sent in for this kind of review, there was no question *if* you should remain. It was just *sign electronically here*, which was just a swipe of your thumbprint. Turning the screen to him for his signature, the major waited for Bishop's response.

For his part, he sat there staring at the screen. Never before had he let his mind wander to this moment. He was certain that if he did, it would distract him, and distractions got his men killed. Clearing his throat, he braced his hands on his knees but never took his eyes off the screen.

After observing Bishop, the major removed his glasses and directly stared at Bishop.

"Captain, you've served your country well. It's time you went home and used that degree you earned eight years ago. You've done your job. Your country is thankful for your service." He thrust his hand out to Bishop then.

Bishop looked at it, and just before too much time lapsed into awkwardness, he shook his hand with a firm grip and then swiped his thumb.

He was going home. The problem was, Bishop had no idea what that meant anymore.

Unlike Roger Tildon, Bishop had never dated in college and never had a long relationship with a steady girlfriend before he was drafted. His family was destroyed. His father had died of a heart attack shortly after he'd been drafted, and his mother and sister lived somewhere with her new husband in Seattle—a place Bishop had no desire to revisit.

Roger had two more years to go. And when Bishop told him he was being shipped back, Roger went too, but only for a short time, to visit with his family on leave. He would return for two more years of battle. At least that's what they thought at the time.

Both of them flew home into Spokane International Airport. Roger went to his family waiting for him at the baggage claim. He'd twirled around a lovely redhead in his arms and then lifted a boy waiting for him who resembled Roger in miniature right down to the brown eyes. "Bishop!" Roger called as he was leaving through the exit. "I want you to meet my family."

Waving, Bishop said, "I've got to run. Someone's waiting. I'll catch up later."

Bishop left and took a cab all the way to Post Falls, Idaho. Once there, he stayed in a hotel for a few days, literally remaining in the hotel room. The trip through the airports and travel was too much. Every loud noise made his pulse race. He found himself reaching for his nonexistent M4 consistently and finding he wasn't even armed for the first time in eight years. The absence of a weapon, on his person, was unnerving.

He finally caught up with Roger a few days later in Coeur d'Alene, Idaho, just a couple miles from Post Falls. They went fishing in the glistening streams. It was quiet in the woods; only the noise of animals alerted him. He felt peaceful there. "What are you going to do now, Bishop? Now that you're *free*?" Roger said as if he'd served a prison sentence instead of a stint in the military.

"I, ah, haven't really thought about it, yet," Bishop said as they walked through a shallow stream keeping their gear high above their heads and out of the water.

Roger stopped midstream. His voice, loud over the din of rushing water, "I know you, man. You need to be needed. Why don't you settle somewhere nearby and keep an eye on my wife and kid? I'm sure you could get on with Idaho State College…maybe teach the weather to some naïve college kids or something."

Like yesterday, Bishop remembered the warm sun on Roger's face through the trees. He'd only smiled and nodded to Roger's suggestion. He wasn't sure about the 'need to be needed' part, but he certainly liked the area.

Later, Roger showed him where he lived.

Two weeks after that, Roger was gone again, and Bishop found himself camping in the same forest Roger introduced him to. After he opened a storage unit to put his spare belongings in, he never left.

Chapter 7

"Mom!" Ben shouted from her bedroom where he was snuggled up under her thick down comforter to keep warm.

"Yes, dear?" she replied as she looked through the pantry in the kitchen, searching for something to make for dinner sans the power.

"When is the electricity going to come back on?"

"I don't know, honey. I'm sure they're working on the lines. There's a lot of snow on the ground so they have a hard time repairing them; it might take a few days."

"It's getting colder," he said in protest to her answer.

Walking back through the house toward the living room, Maeve looked at the smoldering embers in the fireplace and then glanced to her decorative brass firewood rack and said, "Dang it. We're out already. I wish that wood fairy would come back. Oh well, so be it. I shouldn't depend on anyone else anyway."

She climbed the stairs to her bedroom to try and comfort Ben and glanced out of the living room window to see a path going through the freshly fallen snow leading to her front porch. Her pulse quickening, she walked over to the window and looked around. After scanning all around her immediate area, she glanced directly underneath the window. To her surprise, Maeve saw what she had just wished for: a small pile of firewood neatly stacked and ready to be carried inside.

"So he makes day deliveries as well. Hmmm. Why didn't he knock on the door?" Looking around at the swaying trees, she worried about him out there being exposed to elements just to bring her firewood. *He could have at least come in for a cup of coffee to warm up.*

"Mom? Can I put on more clothes?" Ben yelled down the stairs.

She laughed out loud. She had a history of trying to keep Ben in his clothing—he always argued with her when the time came to wear coats and gloves and other outerwear. The boy would often want to wear shorts to school in the dead of an average winter like some of the other locals around town who wore Bermuda shorts in January. She'd never understood the logic in that. "Of course," she yelled back upstairs.

As she met him upstairs he zoomed down the hallway to his own room—to procure another sweatshirt, she imagined. He'd opened his bedroom door, and the air in the hallway was like ice, having suddenly displaced some of the warmth from upstairs. Soon Ben reemerged holding a large navy sweatshirt from his drawer and closed his bedroom door. "I'm going to warm this up by the woodstove before I put it on."

"OK, knock yourself out. Just don't put the shirt on the woodstove, please. The last thing we need is a fire."

As he descended the stairs, she couldn't help but wonder if perhaps they should move into the living room downstairs and block off all the upper bedroom doors to conserve heat. With that idea in mind, she began collecting blankets, pillows, and what she needed from the bathroom for both her and her son. Closing the door behind her, she glanced at the photo on her nightstand, in a way saying goodbye to Roger's image for a few days. Perhaps an absence would do her some good.

She carried her load down the stairs and dropped the bedding on the couch, then put the bathroom essentials into their proper place in the bathroom on the main floor. "We're going to close off the upstairs for now to conserve our heat down here. It'll be an adventure," she said to Ben, who was looking at her for an explanation. "Like camping out."

"OK, that's a good idea, Mom."

He was game. She hoped she could keep up the spirit of adventure because something told her things were about to get really tough. She'd foolishly limited their food supply by negligence and routine. So now she tried to look ahead to prepare for what might come. What worried her most was what would become of them in a few days once all the food ran out. What if she couldn't get to the store?

They certainly couldn't walk that far. They could last a few days, and she'd already decided she would skip her own lunches to conserve food for Ben. In the pit of her stomach, she was afraid she'd already failed her son.

How foolish I've been. I might have doomed us already.

Chapter 8

Bishop's little place in the woods consisted of a fortified lean-to against a stone wall that led inside a cave. He was sure when scouting out a permanent residence in the forest that this spot was favored by the local bears, but after several days of surveillance, none of them ever showed up, so Bishop made the hideout his own. He'd added finesse to the structure over time, picking up pieces of scrap here and there.

Bishop also used his bank account to purchase a few items in town and utilized the scrapyard for the rest. He didn't need much, just a safe place to lay his head in the four years since returning. At some point he thought he might return to society, but the very thought of leaving the peacefulness of his current surroundings made him slink further within its confines. Part of the reason for that was the fact that he'd never let his family know that he returned from war. And now that it had been four years, there was little point in explaining *why*. Bishop was a different man now, and he'd never return to being the same person he was before. No ambition came to him to look for a job in weather or anything else or to reunite with his family. He only wanted to remain alone.

The drip-dripping was a constant sound in the cave depths unless the ground was frozen, as the current conditions were now. The silence brought on by the sudden cold temperatures was eerie. Bishop found himself struggling to even sleep in such a vacuum. Even the unseen wild animals were spooked. He'd awoken twice last night after hearing noise he usually didn't pay much attention to.

It was so quiet that even a passing elk alerted him to his presence. The beasts often traveled in herds, but this one, a young one, must have strayed from the group. The animal's hoofprints still showed his path the next morning. That's when Bishop thought the time was right to take him if he could still find him.

Bagging meat was an all-day job, and he wasn't exactly ready for the hard work, but he suspected the Tildons needed the meat if Maeve was as prepared on the inside as he viewed the outside of their home to be. He'd bet she hardly had any food in the pantry if he looked.

Packing his bow, he also brought along an AR-10 with .308 soft-point rounds if the bow somehow failed him. Bishop wore an extra insulated jacket since overnight more than ten inches of snow had fallen. The added benefit was the relief that Maeve Tildon wouldn't be going anywhere today either. By now she'd discovered her car didn't work, and she was probably panicking about her circumstances.

Bishop turned and, as he always did, locked the metal gate that he had fastened to the structure to deter the temptation of theft from bear or human beast if they happened to stumble upon his little abode. No key was needed. All he needed to do was slide his thumbprint over the touchpad, though taking off a glove was a hindrance in the cold weather. At least he never lost his keys. The solar powered lock worked on minimal sunlight, and that was a good thing since it existed deep in a forest.

Bishop had to break through the snow on his way out of camp. Ten inches of snow would make the day arduous while tracking the elk, but if his hunch was right, the wildlife in the region would soon become scarce from overhunting as food ran low.

Watching the night skies was a habit, and Bishop was confident that what he'd studied and written his thesis on in college was coming true. The Maunder Minimum was upon them, and these low temperatures, so early in the year, were here to stay, and they were only just the beginning.

Chapter 9

Just before dawn the next morning, Maeve stirred, blinking her eyes in the milky blueness of a dawn too early for such a name. Yes, she was awake and could sleep no more. The air of the room was frigid as she stared up at the vaulted ceiling—the realization finally hitting her that with all the empty space above, the precious heat was fleeting too quickly into the void.

She'd slept alongside her child on a neat pallet near the woodstove and without the furnace working. She'd become a wood-feeding slave to provide the warmth needed to keep them comfortable which made her appreciate her elders' plight in days gone by.

As Ben snored, she folded the blankets tightly against his small back as she sat up and stretched out her long legs after keeping them tucked closely underneath herself last night. Her calf muscles were stiff, so she reached for her toes within her thick woolen socks and pulled her muscles stretched and taut. Her long, lean frame allowed her to nearly reach her nose to her knees. She lifted her knees back and forth a few times to prolong the stretch.

After a few seconds, Maeve stood and padded into the kitchen by the dim blue morning light shining through the windows. She resisted the urge to light a candle, preserving the few she had for the darkness of night. She needed to get used to the pale light of day instead of illuminating the room with a flick of a switch. Then, out of habit, she flipped the Keurig switch on, and when there was no sound indicating the water was heating for her, she regained the recollection that things were not as they used to be; there was no power, there was little food, and again she called herself a fool.

"How am I going to deal without coffee? Oh man, no *coffee*, no heat, no food?" she whined out loud. As weary as she sounded, she looked back into the living room and spied the bundle on the floor near the glow of the fire. Her son...she had Ben. She had everything she needed.

Coffee can wait, she thought. The house was quieter than she'd ever remembered it being. The refrigerator no longer hummed; there was a break in the wind and near tons of fallen snow. Neither the settling of the foundation nor water running through pipes made the slightest of sounds. It was as if everything was halted, perhaps just for her, at this moment.

She'd bought this place with Roger brand-new before the humming refrigerator was delivered, before the settling of beams. She'd walked in with him before the builder had arrived to explain the place. She knew this was to be her place before they'd even decided to buy the house. She saw herself here with Roger before Ben was even conceived. The rooms called to her; the surrounding land wanted her here. It was home the second she stepped over the threshold.

Now this place was a sanctuary for her even though memories of Roger were here as well. Her father thought she might take Ben and move home to Maine after Roger's death. He thought perhaps life would be too hard to remain in a place with so many reminders of her dead husband. He offered to let her and Ben move in with him in Maine in her childhood home, but she only said, "This *is* our home. My life is here. I can't imagine leaving." So she'd stayed, and she didn't regret that decision—not then and not since. She thought she might in time, but not yet. She felt grounded here on the edge of the Kootenai National Forest.

Thinking of her father—*he must be worried*—she reached for her iPad. She'd charged the device before the storm and checked her e-mail. As she suspected, there were a few e-mails from family and friends reaching out in shared catastrophe. Her father said that, in Maine, the snow was halfway up the garage door and that her brother had slipped on the ice and wrecked his truck though no real harm was done. She was to call and check in with him as soon as possible.

Elizabeth, her business neighbor, mentioned her husband had slipped and had a concussion. The state of the local hospital was alarming when they'd arrived. Luckily someone was able to stitch the gash in her husband's head, and instead of waiting around in the standing-room-only area they opted to leave and recover at home. "Avoid the hospital at all costs," she wrote, "unless absolutely necessary."

There were a few more relatives' inquiries, but the one that caught her eye was her aunt in Texas saying that the many local migrant workers were returning to warmer grounds in south Mexico due to the ruined orchards and cold weather.

After scanning a few more e-mails, Maeve returned her father's message and let him know she and Ben were totally fine. They had the advantage of wood in their backyard to keep warm. She neglected to tell him about their lack of food, but she didn't want to worry her father any more than she had to.

Then Maeve tuned to the news app, reading that the entire country was engulfed in the severe *cold* crisis. She slid her finger up the screen and found on further inspection that this was a *global* catastrophe.

Meteorologists from around the world had collaborated and found no end to the record-breaking temperatures. NOAA called the weather phenomena a *catastrophe in the making*. The Maunder Minimum had struck even though the phenomenon had only been a debated theory years before, much like climate change and the ethics surrounding stem cell use.

One article predicted famine in the coming weeks of the mini ice age with the calculation of food shortages in the long term and distribution problems in the short.

Looting was expected in the next day or two as stores' stocks began to dwindle to empty metal shelves. Not only that, but the deep freeze affected the war effort abroad. That was one subject Maeve no longer cared to hear about. After the death of her husband, she just didn't care who won or who lost. The war had taken so much from her and her son that nothing else mattered. Not a battle won, a secret obtained, or an island conquered counted more than robbing her and her son of Roger. There was no cause in her mind that warranted his loss.

Maeve set the iPad on the counter after turning the device completely off to preserve the battery and ran her hands briskly over her shoulders, attempting to warm them from a sudden chill through her long-sleeved cotton Henley. She gazed out the frosted window, lost in thought and worry. Then finally she stepped away from the kitchen window as well since the icy air felt as if it was pouring freely through the glass panes. Then she had an idea and quickly grabbed a few decorative pillows from the living room sofa and brought them into the kitchen. Looking around, she realized she could stuff more blankets and pillows against the windows as insulation. That would be a task to accomplish for the day.

"Looting? I'd better get the Glock handgun Roger picked out for me and make sure it's ready. Just in case something happens. I should have already thought of that," she said to herself, always feeling one step behind. Maeve ran up the stairs to retrieve the weapon locked in a biosafe in her nightstand drawer.

Chapter 10

Tracking a young elk through deep snow on uneven terrain took a lot of energy, especially when trying to stay downwind of the animal. And trudging over ten inches of snow on steep slopes wouldn't be safe on the back of his horse. This was one trip Bishop would do by himself.

Having memorized the forest's intricate paths over the past four years through all kinds of weather and forest fires—a yearly occurrence, especially in the summer months—Bishop knew every tree, bush, and stream; every boulder and ravine; and even a few of the bears and mountain lions by name.

The aroma of burning pine wood permeated the area. He'd noticed a sharp increase in the odor over the last few days. Since the power went out, people were relying heavily on their fireplaces for the first time in recent history. No longer was it nostalgic to light up the fireplace: it was a necessity. He wondered how long it would take them to run out of their meager piles before going for the green stuff lying around readily on the forest floor, the likes of which would cause them chimney fires in no time as the creosote built up along the walls. No, these people might live in the woods, but they didn't know how to survive in the woods. And they would soon find out what they were made of when nature put them to the test.

He'd already traveled over three miles, and his eyes were beginning to lose their focus on the two-tone world of white with its few sparse coal projections. When he came upon his intended prey, too afraid to whisper the words out loud, which might spook the animal, he said them within, "Hello, buddy." Bishop raised the bow while the elk stood and pawed at the snowy ground in an effort to get to the dry grass underneath. He aimed the broad head of the arrow at the side of the creature, near the heart, and let loose.

The animal began to bolt from an enemy unheard, but the broad head of the arrow opened a decent-sized hole in the animal's essential organs and dropped him to the ground, dead almost instantly. The kill was swift, and Bishop was thankful that he hadn't tortured the animal or had to track a suffering creature for miles farther.

Upon approach, he knelt in the snow, removed his glove, and ran his hand over the animal's fawn-to-rich-brown fur. To him, each being was special and though he needed meat to survive like most people, sporting for an animal bothered him. Doing so was a waste of life. When he could, he used every part of the beast to honor the animal's existence.

Bishop could tell it was a young elk by his size and by the few points on the small rack that crowned his head. Unsheathing his knife at his side, he pulled out several bags from his pack as well as a tarp to make the job easier and cleaner. He set to work and took the hindquarters, neck meat, and back straps. After nearly half an hour, Bishop packed up all the meat he could carry and left a steaming mound of entrails for the local wildlife to savor. If he passed the same area within three weeks, only bleached bones would remain, and even then the animal itself would return to the earth in time.

Bishop set out again, his legs burning and his pack overburdened with over seventy-five pounds of meat, but his efforts would keep Roger's widow and the boy alive for a time; when the weather was too cold to hunt, they would still have meat if they used the gift wisely.

Struggling up an incline going back the way he'd come, Bishop adjusted his pack on his shoulders and looked up at the afternoon sky. The sun shone weakly through a veil, its outline as small as the moon's. This veil was something he was sure would seem thicker in the months ahead, as if the sun had absconded from man, fleeing for a time and taking with it the warmth of life. He predicted not all would survive. In fact, only a few, if he was right. The thought of the ravages men had ahead of them saddened him.

As Bishop continued back to his cabin struggling ever more with the weight upon his back, he contemplated the best way to handle delivering the meat. Stopping first to saddle Jake, his horse, to help with the trek to Maeve's, he could drop the pack on her porch after dark, but he wasn't sure if she'd discover the meat in time and that could attract unwanted predators to her location.

In fact, the more he thought about how to deliver the goods, he found no way to avoid actually talking to her. He'd been eluding conversation with the wood deliveries. Part of him wanted to have a real conversation with the redheaded widow, but the other part of him did not. However, at the end of his argument with himself, he fell on the idea that taking care of them was a duty he owed to Roger.

She probably didn't even know how to butcher the meat, and he needed to get into the house anyway because he had a new deadbolt to replace the flimsy lock on the back door. Also, he needed to see if she had snow tires in the garage that could replace the low-tread wheels on her FJ before he sought out new ones. That task alone would take part of the evening, and that was only if she let him inside the door to begin with.

Chapter 11

By sundown, Maeve had most of the first-floor windows covered in an extra layer of protection against the cold. Upstairs, she'd closed all of the doors and used towels or clothing to block the warm air from escaping under the doorframes. Even the drains in the sinks drafted cold air into the rooms, so she cut up a rubber mat to cover the holes when not in use. Once she was finished trying to insulate the house from the frigid outdoors, she heard a knock on the front door.

"Someone's at the door, Mom," Ben said as he sat up from playing with his cars on the living room floor.

Maeve left the kitchen and said on her way to the door, "I don't know who would be out in this weather. It's way below freezing out there." She reached for her pistol on the high shelf of the hall closet on her way to the door. Ben watched her in surprise as she handled the Glock 17. She put up a silent finger to her mouth to usher him into quietness.

Holding the gun behind her back, Maeve peeked through the peephole in the door to see who was on the other side. She saw him standing there, the man who secretively delivered wood stacks to her door, the one her son called *the hermit*.

"I've got to ask him his name," she whispered.

"What, Mom? Who is it?" Ben asked.

Without answering her son's question, she said, "Ben, can you go in the kitchen for me and stay out of sight?"

"Why, Mom?" he said, looking confused.

The guy knocked again, and she jumped this time. She let out a frustrated breath and then opened the door a crack. The brisk, cold wind invaded her home.

He stood there with his pack weighed down and dressed in insulated camouflage as if he'd never left the war. He stared right through her with those blue eyes and dirty light-blond hair. The beard on his face gave him a wild man look, though the eyes were gentle. She would have feared him if it weren't for the eyes as blue as glacier ice. His complexion was weathered too, and she could tell he'd once been an attractive man; he still was, but in a torn and rugged way.

The frigid air passed freely inside, and he suddenly said, "Don't open your door to strangers, Maeve." His statement came out harsh, a condemnation of her actions.

"I…I know who you are."

"You can't do that. It's not safe," he said, frustrated.

"I have a gun."

He shook his head. "Don't tell anyone you have a gun. Don't say the words."

She couldn't believe he was giving her a hard time.

"What do you want?"

"I have something for you…and the boy."

"What is it? We don't need anything…"

His eyes stared through her again, and she knew he doubted her words.

"Elk meat. Do you know how to butcher it out?"

"Ugh…I'm sure I can manage. Thank you." She opened the door wide for him to step inside.

"Don't let anyone into your home," he said in an urgent warning and then spied the boy peeking around the corner at him. She turned and saw Ben waving at the hermit.

"Well, you might as well come inside. I doubt you'd hurt us. Besides, you're letting all the cold air in with the door open." She found she was shaking already with the freezing air engulfing her.

He must have noticed because he stepped inside, and she took two big steps backward with the Glock still behind her back. He closed the door behind himself and bolted the lock, and when he stood right in front of her, she realized he loomed over her and was at least six feet tall. He'd taken the heavy pack off his back and stretched and then looked at her and the boy as if he was assessing them.

"Always use the deadbolt, even during the day now. It's not safe. Anyone can get through with one kick."

His voice, she thought, was deep and wounded even though he was using it to condemn her now. She nodded that she should keep the door bolted.

He removed his snow-covered coat and hung it near the door and removed his knit hat. His hair stood out all over. He untied his boots and left them on the tile to drain as the ice melted and puddled all over. As he warmed, she noticed an odor coming from him. A mix of sweat and something else. She was sure he wasn't one to bathe every day considering he lived in the woods. He didn't smell filthy, just like a man who'd worked all day from sunup to sundown. She remembered Roger smelling the same way after working out or coming home from a long run.

He stood there in his stocking feet waiting for her to usher him inside further. Then he said, "Can you show me to the kitchen? I'll help you get this parceled out."

She didn't say anything or move a muscle. She wasn't sure she wanted him in her house, but then again something inside of her didn't want him to leave, either. He was protective. He was strong, and something in her trusted the man even though she shouldn't.

A slight smile pulled up the corner of his lips. "You can hold the gun on me the whole time if you think that will make you feel safer. I'm not going to hurt you or your son."

She'd forgotten she had the Glock in her hand, but he hadn't. The hand holding the gun, moved down to her thigh so that it was in plain view at her side.

He looked at the Glock 17 and then looked her in the eyes again. "Do you know how to fire that weapon?"

She nodded.

He looked skeptical.

"The kitchen is this way," Ben interrupted, and the visitor looked at the small boy before he followed him from the foyer, stepping around Maeve as he did.

Maeve shook her head but followed the guys into the kitchen after putting the handgun back in the closet.

"What's your name?" Ben asked the hermit.

Maeve watched as he set the pack down against the kitchen cabinet carefully. The bundle must weigh a ton, though he lifted it with ease. He turned on the water to let the tap warm, but even with a gas furnace only cold water ran out.

"Sorry, we ran out of hot water," Maeve said.

Bishop used the nearby soap to wash his hands anyway. He looked at the boy while he washed and said, "My name's Bishop. What's yours?"

"I'm Ben, and that's my mom, I mean…"

She stepped forward behind her son. "I'm Maeve Tildon."

"Yes, I know your names," Bishop said.

"Bishop knew your dad, Ben," she said, not wanting her son to think she would just let any hermit or stranger into their home.

"He did?" Ben asked, but Bishop let his silence be his answer.

Maeve caught his reluctance to speak about Roger, but Ben did not. Perhaps that's why Bishop was a hermit. He didn't want to talk about anything to do with the war, not even Roger.

"Do you have a sharp knife?" Bishop asked.

"Yes," she said and quickly rummaged around the kitchen to find her best tool for the job. She also retrieved a box of resealable bags to use and a marker to label the packages with.

"We were beginning to run out of food. My car isn't working either, so this is very kind of you. We're also out of power, so I can't put them in the freezer. Can I keep the meat outside?" Maeve asked, trying to find a solution.

"No. Someone will take the meat, and the smell will attract the wildlife. Not safe to keep outside."

"Where can I put it then?"

"In a cooler in the garage where the temperature is still well below freezing," he said as he dried his hands on a towel.

"Can I get you something to drink before you start?"

"Water, please."

Maeve rolled up her sleeves and washed her hands too after she gave him the glass, which he drank straight down at once.

Then Ben pulled himself up on the barstool so that he could watch what was going on.

Bishop looked for a knife sharpener from the drawer where Maeve retrieved the knife, but there wasn't one in sight, so he opened a cupboard and grabbed a ceramic mug, the big kind that a devout coffee lover would continuously refill.

She watched him as he flipped the cup over and ran the flat side of the blade against the exposed stone. He did this a few times on each side and tested the edge again. He seemed satisfied with the sharper blade then and opened the pack of elk.

Pulling out a clear bag with two long strips of meat, Bishop rinsed them under cold water and then patted them dry with clean towels that she'd laid out for him. He began slicing the lengths into small steaks about an inch apart, and Maeve picked them up and put them into the smaller bags, sealing them inside with as little air as possible. When they were done with those, she retrieved a large clean blue cooler from the garage and had Ben put the finished steaks inside.

She kept out one set of steaks for their dinner later that night. Though they would have meat to eat and beans that she'd cooked on the woodstove, there were no other vegetables to go along with their meal. She had a feeling that the lack of vegetables would be an issue they would have to contend with until this weather thing passed over or when she could get to the store.

"Um, do you know anything about cars? My truck isn't starting, and I need to go get some supplies before this gets too bad." He shifted his weight from one foot to the other but instead of answering handed her a few more steaks. Maeve slid them into the next bag and wrote on the label, then gave the package to Ben to put in the cooler. She wasn't sure why he had not answered her question. "I mean, if it's not too much of a problem for you to check the truck out while you're here."

"I'll look at it. Do you have snow tires somewhere?"

"Snow tires? Yes, they're in the garage stacked in the corner. I know it's a lot to ask. You must be exhausted after bringing this to us."

"That's all right. I'll take a look at it when I'm finished here, but you really shouldn't drive around with that truck. It needs to be locked up in the garage and out of sight. I also brought a deadbolt for your back door."

She looked at Ben before asking the question on her mind. Scaring her son was something she was trying to avoid. "Do you think we'll get looters as far as up here? I mean, we know a lot of our neighbors. I can't imagine they're the type of people to steal from others."

Bishop continued to slice easily through the meat and divide up what he could as quickly as possible. She thought he was probably used to being alone and wasn't used to so much conversation at once.

He seemed to wait longer than the social norm to respond to her questions, perhaps trying to formulate his response using the least number of words.

"Desperate people are dangerous. They do things you couldn't imagine."

His expression told her more than the words, as if he too were trying to limit the fear in front of her son. A tingle of fright ran up her spine.

"So you think this will get worse?"

Again, he didn't respond for a while. "Don't open the doors when someone knocks. I'll check on you every few days."

That certainly wasn't enough to stave off her fears. In fact, she was more terrified than before. Not only that, the room had become quite dark with the waning light fading through the blocked windows. She lit several candles so that they could see as they worked.

"Surely this will blow over in a few days," she said and smiled at Ben.

"It won't," he said, shaking his head while handing her a few more steaks to package.

"What do you mean?"

"We're in the Maunder Minimum—for years now. This will go on for at least ten years if we're lucky. The last time this happened, the ice age lasted seventeen years."

Ben piped up, "Ice age? Like when the mammoths were here?"

"Yes," Bishop said, nodding. He was working diligently while answering when asked, though a little delayed. He looked healthy enough, but she knew he was scarred by war or at least suspected that was the case.

Once he'd finished boning out the last hindquarter, his arms were completely bloodied. Bishop washed them in the frigid water from the tap and then moved the heavy chest full of elk steaks out to the garage while Maeve held a flashlight to guide the way. It was completely dark outside by then. He set the chest next to the inside wall of the garage. "The tires are over there," she said and flashed the beam in the corner of the garage.

He nodded and then stepped inside the house next to her and closed and locked the door to the garage. "Keep this door locked all the time, too. Even when you're inside," he said.

Nodding, she replied, "Um, would you like to take a shower while you're here? The water's cold, but you could clean up, and I'll make the steaks. The least I could do is feed you for all of this work you've done for us."

He didn't delay in his response this time. "No," he said and stepped around her.

"O...kay," she said, following him back to the kitchen where she found him cleaning the knife he'd used with care.

It wasn't that he was rude before, she thought, *but how do I communicate with this guy?* Maeve began cleaning up their mess with hot, soapy water that she'd heated on the woodstove, scrubbing the counter free of blood.

"Do you have extra 9mm ammunition for the Glock?" Bishop said, interrupting her thoughts.

She looked up at him with a blank stare. "Uh, I think there's some bullets in a box upstairs."

He let out a somewhat frustrated breath.

"I'm sorry, I didn't pay attention to this kind of thing. Roger took care of all of that."

He nodded as if he understood. "Still, you need to keep the ammunition with the weapon, near you at all times, so that you don't have trouble getting to it in a time of crisis. I can clean the Glock and show you how to reload the magazine and make sure it's in good working order while I'm here if you'd like."

It was the most words he'd strung together at one time, and Maeve stood there with her mouth slightly open when just earlier she'd been pondering how to deal with the man of few words. *So he can talk...* She smiled at him and said, "Yes, please. Honestly, I know next to nothing about the weapon, though Roger took me out to the range several times." Finding him staring right into her eyes, she had to look away. "He just always took care of the maintenance. I don't even know how to load the magazine."

"It's no problem. I'll show you. The fact that you know it's a magazine instead of a clip, is a good thing." With his voice lower than before, she realized he too had a difficult time remembering or talking about Roger.

"I'll be right back then," she said, dropping the cleaning towel on the counter. She ran upstairs to retrieve the kit Roger kept for her Glock and the few boxes of the 9mm bullets she had in her possession.

When she returned, she found Bishop had knelt down with Ben in the living room, showing her son how to fix the axle of one of his toy trucks. "See, you can snap it back into place if you push right there."

"It hurts my thumb when I try," Ben said.

"Then use something like the edge of the bricks near the woodstove to add more force. Go ahead and try."

She waited before interrupting them. Rare was it that her son had a man like his father around, and Bishop was the closest possible person fitting that description.

Taking his toy truck to the woodstove, Ben held the axle in place and levered the metal bar over the opening of the tight plastic axle. He used his hands to push down and leaned in to add more force. An audible snap was heard, and he quickly picked up and turned over the truck and spun the wheel. He beamed. "Hey, thanks! It worked."

"Don't thank me. You did all the work, buddy."

Then something miraculous happened. The corners of Bishop's mouth turned up as Ben gave him a high five. *The man can smile.*

The fact that instead of quickly fixing the toy he took the time to teach her son how to fix it himself was endearing. If she'd had doubts about inviting Bishop into her home before, she no longer did now.

As her son rolled the repaired red truck over the rug, she brought Bishop the cleaning kit and bullets for her handgun.

They sat at the kitchen table as he showed her how to release the magazine and unloaded the weapon. Then she watched as he cleaned and oiled it, taking care to answer any of her questions. Finally, he showed her how to reload the magazine. And like her son's dilemma with the truck axle, she had a hard time popping the bullets into the magazine very well with her slender fingers.

Though, this time, he had no easy tips. "You'll have to work at it. Get used to the feel of sliding them in. Practice," he said as he stood and then went to the front door and put on his outerwear and boots.

"Are you going already?" Ben ran up and asked him.

"Honey, if Bishop needs to go, we won't delay him. He was very kind to bring us the elk meat."

"I'm going to change the tires and take a look at your mom's truck, and then you can help me with changing the lock on the back door," he said to Ben, who looked elated with the prospect of helping him.

"My keys are right there on the side table," Maeve said.

"Keep these hidden," he said to her, and by now she was used to him warning her about what to do. She smiled at him and nodded while she continued to clean up the kitchen.

The last thing he said as he went through the garage door was to Ben. "Always lock this door with the deadbolt to keep you and your mom safe inside." He knelt down to Ben's level. "You're old enough to do that now. Keep the doors bolted at all times. That's your job, OK?"

Ben nodded with a somber expression. "I will."

For a minute as she watched the two, it was like Roger was here again, and she had to push that image away quickly. Bishop was not Roger. Roger always had a perpetual smile on his face, and Bishop wore the opposite most of the time. No doubt that was probably a result of the war, and had Roger returned, she was sure he too would have lost his smile, but in time she would have helped him find it again.

Bishop stood and patted Ben on the head. His eyes were sad as he went back through the garage door.

She heard him lift the garage entrance manually and rummage around in there.

Meanwhile, she warmed a cast-iron skillet on the woodstove and cooked two of the steaks, seasoning them with only a little salt and pepper. She'd added another log to the fire, and soon the smell of frying meat permeated their senses. When Bishop arrived earlier, they'd not even had lunch, and now it was already dinnertime.

Ben was trying to sneak peeks at Bishop through a crack in the window while she cooked.

"Is he still out there?" Maeve asked him, though she had no idea how he could see in the pitch dark.

"Yeah, he's working on the tires. I can only tell because of the flashlight moving around once in a while."

By the time the steaks were done, she had heard the engine to her FJ start outside. He pulled the truck into the garage, and then she heard the rattling sound of him closing the garage door again. She had no doubt he wouldn't forget to latch the door manually as well.

He came through the door leading into the house and handed her the keys to her FJ. "It's running fine now. The engine was probably just cold. I put it in the garage," he said and then picked up his pack and pulled out a deadbolt lock with a set of keys and headed to her back door off of the kitchen with Ben trailing him.

He soon pulled out a multiuse tool that she thought he must have brought along with him and replaced the flimsy lock with the deadbolt. Ben watched him the whole time, and Bishop handed him things to hold for him as he worked quickly and carefully to keep the cold air out of the house.

When he was finished and was about to leave, he said, "Maeve, if you're going to go somewhere, please don't go far, and do it tomorrow but no later than that. After tomorrow, even your kind neighbors, those you've known since you moved here, will start to become desperate, and desperate people are very dangerous. I'll be around. I'll check on you and Ben in a few days."

Those words of warning made her stomach tighten. She was just beginning to become scared before he came, and now she was utterly scared through and through, and perhaps that was his point. She should be afraid. Fear enabled survival; that was a concept she was learning.

"All right. What if…what if something happens and I—we—need your help before you check in on us?" She felt stupid for uttering those words as soon as they left her mouth.

"I'll be back," he said and opened the back door and shut it just as quickly to keep the cold outside in the dark with him. Ben rushed over to the door and locked the deadbolt behind him. Her son was now the keeper of the house locks and seemed to take the job seriously.

She stood there silently for a moment watching the locked door and looked down to the tile where the marks from his boots were the only proof he'd been there.

"I'm hungry, Mom," Ben said, and she was too. Her stomach growled in protest of the savory aroma, and yet she knew Bishop had to have been starving but still wouldn't share this meal with them when she'd asked.

"OK," she said. Near the woodstove, Maeve served their simple dinner of elk steaks and pinto beans, which turned out to be a feast for kings.

Chapter 12

Beginning the long trudge back to camp, Bishop untethered Jake from the back of Maeve's property. He didn't think the boy had spotted the horse hitched just past the tree line. He found himself taking in deep breaths of sharp cold air as he rode back to camp.

Being in Roger's house brought back many memories. He'd noticed the pictures on the walls of his friend holding his newborn son, of Roger in uniform soon after recommission, of Roger at his wedding with Maeve in her dress. It was as if he just lost his friend, not knowing until recently that Roger had died over there like so many others.

Bishop had died over there, in a way. Part of him had at least, and he knew he would never be the man he once was. He would take care of Roger's family and do his best to ensure they survived this. He owed him that.

When he arrived in camp, it was snowing again, adding yet more on top of what would eventually compact and become ice; it wouldn't melt, not for a long time. All the snow that fell now would become another layer to dig out of for years to come. They would have to continue to dig in order to survive.

He dismounted from Jake and led him into the makeshift stable. Bishop was cold and hungry and so was his horse. He knew Maeve was just kind when she offered the meal and a chance at a real shower, but he couldn't stay there for longer than necessary. There was something about her that bothered him. She was kind and gentle and totally vulnerable there by herself, and Ben was a good kid.

He hated to think what might become of them if someone with bad intentions happened upon them. Even just thinking about the possibility he found his fists balled up in anger.

Bishop laid out feed for Jake and used a clean towel to wipe away the moisture from his hide while he ate. Instead of going down to the stream for water, he scooped up buckets full of clean snow and set it on his kerosene stove to melt. After he had given the first bucket of water to Jake, he continued to add snow to the large pot. When the melted snow had begun to boil, he used some of it to warm a few main entrees of the MREs he had stashed away. Typically, he ate them cold, but for novice partakers of the prepackaged meals, he went the extra step. He didn't even look at the name *du jour* on the package any longer; they all tasted the same. If he didn't have a source of fresh meat or was out of time and hungry like today, he just grabbed one of the hundreds of these he had stashed away in boxes in the cave. Some of them were expired, but he still ate them with no ill effects.

The peanut butter and cracker packages were a treat he often used around midday if he was working especially hard. Otherwise, he seldom ate more than two meals a day.

Once he was finished with his meal, the boiling water had cooled to warm. Bishop removed his clothes. By candlelight, he stood naked near his stove and brought out a bar of soap and a rough hand cloth. He started at the top of his head and first washed the sweat and grime from his hair and face and then worked his way down past the back of his neck and his chest and finished at his feet. His muscles were sore and glistened with moisture in the golden candlelight. Once he had rinsed away the soap, he fished out a new set of clean clothes and dressed in another set of camo pants, clean socks, underwear, and a long-sleeve thermal tee. His metal dog tags were the only thing he wore continuously.

Once dressed, Bishop slipped on his boots once more and scooped more snow into the pot and added his dirty clothes. He didn't care about stains; his only concerns were the germs. Once the water came to a boil, he left them there for another ten minutes and then turned off the heat. Once cool enough, he wrung out each piece and hung them by the woodstove to dry. By morning, they would be stiff as cardboard but sanitized. It was an efficient system he'd developed over time.

Adding another log to the fire in the woodstove, he heated both sides of the cabin wall, the stable lean-to area as well as the inside of his home. Then he slipped inside of his sleeping bag, set up on a cot with his AR-15 by his side, and fell asleep.

A few hours later, Bishop woke to the sounds of the war he once knew. By now, he'd learned to tell the dream to go away no matter the gore he found himself in, whether it was him reliving the time he found a mutilated Chinese child gored by a fellow soldier, her hands clinging to a stuffed bear, or when he discovered that same soldier a day later missing the lower half of his body from a well-placed grenade. None of it ever made any sense to him, and there wasn't a single night that he didn't relive some part of what he'd gone through. The nightmares were always right there waiting for his return, but it was more than that this time.

Now, Bishop was freezing cold in the dream, and when he acknowledged the dream, it began to fade away. First, the blood muted and then the forested terrain gave way to darkness, though the shivering did not. He woke himself and found that not only was he cold, but the temperature had plummeted drastically. Opening his eyes, he discovered white ice crystals had encroached well into his cabin through the cracks in the walls.

"Jeez!" Bishop said, alarmed at the drastic change, and he immediately jumped up from his cot and started a fire in the woodstove that heated both sides of the cabin wall leading to Jake's stable. He quickly put on his outer gear and opened his door, finding another two feet of fresh snow blocking his way to the stable side.

After breaking his way through, knowing his horse was in jeopardy from the extreme temperatures, he found Jake lying on his side, ice crystals formed around his muzzle near the warmest corner of the stable.

"Get up, buddy," he urged the animal. Urging him to walk and move his blood through his arteries was the only way to save the animal. If he let him lie there, he would surely die of exposure in no more than an hour's time. "Damn, I should have known better," Bishop cursed to himself.

Then he thought of Maeve and Ben. If only he'd known the temperature would make such a drastic drop he would have prepared them, but right now they were more than likely all right since she'd had the woodstove going when he left. It was near morning outside, just barely; only a faint moon lit the sky behind the clouds.

He pulled on Jake's harness and had to yell, "Get up, Jake!" Only then did the animal finally make the effort to do so. He wasn't steady on his legs either. Bishop walked him around the small stable to get his blood pumping. When he finally seemed as if he would survive, Bishop gave him a little hay, not enough to fill him full but enough to keep him interested.

Then Bishop went back to his cabin and loaded more wood into the woodstove. Generally, he only fueled it enough to avoid freezing in order to limit the amount of smoke coming from his chimney, but this was unavoidable. He let the wood burn high, and soon the ice crystals that were invading his space began to retreat.

As an additional effort, he grabbed two large stones to heat on the woodstove and then alternated them in Jake's water trough every few hours to keep the water from freezing over. They conducted a lot of heat and helped to keep the stable area warmer as well. Now he saw a need to enclose Jake's stable area completely. The lean-to wasn't going to work in these kinds of temperatures.

As soon as the sun began to rise, Bishop had confined most of the structure so that the snow could not enter by covering every chink in the wood slates with scrap pieces and then tacking a tarp around the exterior. Jake could rest safely from the elements. "There you go, buddy. Not a bad place," he said, and Jake answered him with a shake of his head.

Bishop's last task was assembling a gate, and he was thankful he'd scavenged useful items left in the woods over the years. He was able to build everything from the scraps he'd found.

Once he was finished, he added more wood in the woodstove to keep up with the extreme cold and realized he now would have to continue to keep it going around the clock.

The structure built onto the cave entrance was large enough to fit a woodstove and the kerosene stovetop along one wall and to hang items on pegs on the other side. The chimney was vented through the roof there. The walkway opened to a table area, and then beyond that was the cave room where several cots were lined up. He slept in there, and that was also where he kept all of his supplies.

The only problem with his setup was that there was only one entrance and one exit. That was something that had always bothered him—one should always have more than one exit from any particular dwelling.

By then it was only early evening, and he was wondering how Maeve and young Ben were faring with even colder temperatures and the extra snow on the ground. *She wouldn't try to drive in this deep snow, right? There's no way they cleared the roads.* But his mind kept telling him if there was a will there was a way, and if Maeve wanted to take the truck out to get to the store she probably would have tried to chance the trip no matter the conditions, which worried him.

He found himself saddling up Jake with the excuse that he needed to get the horse moving and told himself he would just swing by Maeve's house to check for tire tracks and come straight back and that was all.

Bishop took a different trail than the one before so that he wouldn't mark a clear path through the trees between her property and his hideout three miles into the woods.

Not long after he set out, he smelled not only pine logs burning but something else as well. It was pitch dark by then, but as he and Jake meandered through the forest, the smell became even stronger. By the time he was only a mile away from camp, he began to see a glow through the trees coming from the direction of Maeve's home.

"Oh no!" he said and urged Jake to hurry through the deep snow. As he traveled closer, he found it wasn't her home set ablaze but that of a nearby neighbor's. He rounded the house in a hurry and found Maeve and Ben standing in the front driveway.

"Ben, get back in the house!" she yelled, and then she looked up at him, startled. She didn't recognize him at first. He pulled his hat away. "It's all right, Maeve. Get inside. I'll go check it out." He could see she was concerned about what was happening to her neighbors a half mile down the road.

"There was a truck there. They had guns. We heard shots. There are children in that house!" she screamed.

"I said get inside the house and lock the doors, Maeve! Do it now!"

He took off as she headed inside. He hated to yell at her, but she wasn't going to listen to him otherwise. He'd seen that same stunned look in soldiers as bullets flew. You had to get their attention and fast, or else they'd die.

From his point of view atop Jake as he neared the burning house, at least three men were pulling items out into the front yard. He stayed just outside the glow of the fire to try and discern what was taking place. That's when he noticed a body of a man out front in the driveway. The snow around his head was crimson red. No doubt he'd been shot execution style.

Maeve had said there were children inside, but he saw no young people around the place.

Bishop crept around the side of a barn. He intended to take the one man on watch by surprise but needed to stash Jake in a safe place. If there were people still inside the house, then they were either dead or dying by now. "Stay right here, Jake," he said as he tethered him to a post safely out of sight. Then he pulled his rifle out of the saddle and slung it by the strap around his back.

Peeking around the side of the barn, he counted again and found only three men, all armed, two of them moving what looked like ammo cans and rifles out of chests they'd hauled from the house and loading them into a pickup truck while the third man stood watch.

"Damn looters already," Bishop whispered and then took advantage of the lookout's damaged peripheral vision. He'd been staring at the fire for some time, and since Bishop knew his field of vision was compromised he ran along the periphery in the pitch dark until he was nearly on top of him.

"Preppers never learn to keep their damn mouths shut," the guy on watch said. "Loose lips sink ships," he said and spit into the snow near the dead man.

Bishop lost all doubts that these people might be the owners upon hearing the leader's slur. The two additional men were still busy loading items into the back of the truck when the spitter said, "Hurry up. It's damn cold out here."

He's right about that much, Bishop thought and then raised his AR, sighted the spitter. He took a breath, let it out and held, then squeezed the trigger. The shot hit the man right in the temple. He never saw it coming and fell to the ground in a heap alongside the owner.

The other two men leaped from the back of the pickup to the other side and took cover. Bishop was already on the move, having anticipated their actions, and ran around the front of the truck before they even had a chance to aim. With two successive shots from his AR, he caught them both—one in the chest and the other in the neck.

Then he heard a child's scream coming from the second floor of the burning house, and when he looked up, he saw a young girl with blond hair standing in a window staring down at him in fear.

"Oh, Jesus!" he screamed and immediately looked for options to get her free. There was no way to enter the house from the front entrance. The entire first floor was engulfed in flames. There was only one way to get to her, so he climbed the outside of the front porch and pulled himself up onto the roof. Since the first floor was an inferno, he knew he was taking a chance with his life and traversed the edge of the building to keep his weight on the outer walls.

He climbed until he was right at the dormer to the girl's window. Looking through the window past the frightened girl, he saw through the smoke that her bedroom door was closed but already on fire. She had stuffed a blanket under the door to keep out the smoke.

"Open the window!" he yelled to her, but she only continued to scream. "Stand back!" he said, but she didn't respond to that either. He had mere seconds before the child would die before his very eyes, so he reached for his knife. With the hilt he pounded through the glass, shattering it everywhere. The fire came alive behind the girl, feeding on the new oxygen immediately, and with one motion, Bishop reached for her, grabbed her, and swung her out into the night and around the side of the house. The fire engulfed the empty space soon after, and Bishop was left with no other option than to fall with the girl to the snowy ground below.

When he did, he landed on his side with glass all around them, and he found the girl was unconscious on top of his chest. He sat up and held her small body in his arms. She had a pulse, but they were both covered in cuts and burns, and the back of his right arm was cut up.

Lifting the girl in his arms as he stood, he noticed she wore a white nightgown singed at the edges. He was sure she'd just lived through horrors no one should see and couldn't help but think maybe perhaps it wasn't *fair* to save her life. *Maeve will know what to do with her.* The child was smaller than Ben and weighed nearly nothing.

Quickly trying to get back to Jake, he passed the truck loaded with supplies from the burning house. Then, out of nowhere, the guy he'd shot in the chest earlier raised his handgun.

With the injured child in his arms, Bishop struggled to grab his AR-15 in time. Instead, he swung his boot when a shot rang out.

Chapter 13

"Mom, what's happening? I'm scared," Ben said as he watched Maeve from near the fireplace. She stared out into the darkness toward the bright flames down the road. There was nothing to see, though. They'd heard a few terrifying shots and then nothing again.

She imagined Bishop's body lying dead out there in the snow, and there was nothing she could do about it. Terrified as her son, Maeve turned to Ben and said, "Son, can you stay right here for me? Don't do anything but sit right there, no matter what you hear. I'll be right back. I'm just going to go down the road a ways to see if I can spot Bishop. Do you hear me? Don't move a single muscle from this spot."

But her son looked up at her with a pleading stare. She was riveted to where she stood. How could she ask this of him, this boy who'd already lost his father?

"Don't go, Mom," he whispered, his face as pale as a ghost's.

She delayed her answer. "I'll only go as far as the driveway. I promise you, I'll be right back. I will *not* leave you." She grabbed her pistol then and didn't look him in the face as she headed toward the door after putting on a black wool coat. "I'll only be a second," she said and drifted quickly through the doorway.

In the pitch dark, her eyes took a minute to adjust and still could only barely make out shadows. Once she traversed through the snow to the end of her driveway, she peeked east around the tree line. Through the glow of the fire beyond, a quarter of a mile down the road, she saw a man on top of a dark horse loping his way toward her.

"Bishop?" she whispered. Whoever it was, he was slumping over, silhouetted with the blaze behind him and bobbing with the horse's slow cadence. She was riveted to her spot behind the pine trunk. *It has to be Bishop.*

If only she could shine her flashlight, she could know for sure, but she was afraid it might be one of the shooters who attacked the house down the road.

The rider neared, and she squatted down with her Glock in her hands. The horse drifted close to her and then stopped.

"Maeve," he said, his voice weak. "I know you're there. Take the child."

Flooded with relief, she wiped her sleeve over her eyes and slid the gun into her big coat pocket while she came out from behind the tree trunk. Nearing the side of the horse, which sniffed her and nudged her shoulder, she nearly cried out when Bishop draped the unconscious child over her arms. Though there was little light, the girl wore a thin white nightgown and showed no signs of life. "Oh my God."

"Hurry, Maeve, get her inside."

She turned and ran for the front door as fast as she could through the thick snow. When she came inside, Ben's eyes were round saucers. "What happened, Mom? Who is that?"

"Get a blanket!" she said and quickly laid the girl on the couch after kicking the door closed behind her.

"Where's Bishop?" Ben asked.

"He should be coming. He was right behind me." The lack of warmth was not the immediate danger to this girl in Maeve's view. She had cuts all over her with glass bits still embedded in her face, neck, and shoulders. Why she was unconscious wasn't immediately clear. There was soot all over her face, and her gown was destroyed with singe marks and blood. She had a pulse and was breathing, but her breath was raspy.

"It's probably smoke inhalation. Oh God, what do I do? Her breathing's too shallow," Maeve said frantically, and Ben looked over her shoulder at the girl.

"That's Louna! Andy's little sister."

Maeve hadn't even thought about who the child was, but Ben was right. *God only knows what happened to the rest of the family.*

She sat the child up and began massaging her back and called her name, hoping she would become conscious. "Louna, Louna, can you hear me?"

"Where's Bishop, Mom?"

Maeve shook her head. "I don't know." She continued to call out to the child in her arms while Ben ran to the door. When he opened it, he yelled, "Mom! He's in the snow! Bishop is lying in the snow next to his horse!"

After laying the girl back down and covering her up, she ran for the open doorway. In the house's ambient light shining out, she saw Bishop sprawled out in the snow next to his horse in the driveway. Beside him, the horse nudged his body with his muzzle.

"Ben, get your coat on. First, unlock the backyard door to the garage. Then, take the horse around the back and lead him inside. Can you do that?"

"Uh, sure," he said. "Is…Bishop dead?"

Not wanting to consider that, she said, "Hurry, I've got to get him inside."

Putting hands underneath his arms, she used all of her strength to drag him across the snow and inside the front door. By the time Ben returned, he helped lift Bishop's legs enough to barely get him through the threshold so that they could close the door. That's when she saw all the blood by the dim light.

"Oh my. I didn't know he'd been shot. Ben, lock the door and get some towels quick!" She checked under his neck for a pulse and found it there, but the wound in his shoulder worried her. Not only that, the back of his right arm was in bad shape with burn marks on his coat sleeve and embedded glass.

Never more in her life did she wish she'd become a nurse instead of an English major than right then. On her knees crouching next to him, she said, "OK, they're both breathing, but he's definitely bleeding. I wonder if the bullet went through." And to find out, she pulled him over and saw there was indeed an exit wound. "That's a good sign, right?" she asked Ben, who stood looking at her, clueless.

He shrugged his shoulders.

She took the stack of towels from him and put a layer under Bishop's shoulder and then pressed down with another layer as hard as she could on the front side. Meanwhile, she looked over at the girl on the couch. "Ben, go check and see if she's breathing, OK?"

He wandered over to the girl in a reluctant stride and put his hand in front of her nose. "I don't feel anything."

"Look and see if her chest is rising with her breaths."

He watched carefully for a few seconds. "Yeah, she's breathing."

She held up two fingers together. "OK, now put your fingers on the underside of her neck, under her jaw, and see if you feel a pulse."

"What's a pulse?" he said, his expression puzzled.

"It's that beat you feel in your wrist and in your neck. It pulses with your heartbeat."

"Oh." He did as he was told and waited.

She was terrified the girl would die right there on her sofa.

Ben's eyes widened, and he nodded. "Yes, I feel it."

"Good, OK. How fast is it beating?"

"Like, *tap, tap, tap*," he said bobbing his head with the rhythm.

"Good, I need you to do that every few minutes for me while I'm trying to help Bishop. If it becomes slower or faster than it is now, tell me quickly, OK?"

Ben nodded that he understood. It was a lot to ask of a six-year-old, but she had no other choice. She couldn't leave Bishop's side at the moment, or he would continue to bleed out.

After another five minutes, she asked Ben to check Louna's pulse again, and he said the beat was the same as before. Then she said, "Now I need to you come and help me with Bishop." Her hands and arms were covered in Bishop's blood by then, and the grout crevices in her tile entryway were filling with rivers of the red blood. "We need to move him somewhere where I can work on him better."

"He's lying on his gun, Mom," Ben said, and in all the confusion she hadn't even noticed that he was, in fact, lying on the the rifle that was slung over his other shoulder.

"Great. OK, that can't be comfortable. I think the bleeding in his shoulder has stopped. Can you clear a spot next to the fire and bring me that large comforter?"

"Sure," Ben said and did as she asked.

Having him near the fire would at least allow her to see the extent of his injuries better since the light was brighter there.

While Ben brought her the comforter, she removed his boots, guns, and knife. Then she laid out the quilt alongside his body. "OK, I can't drag him like I did before or his shoulder will start bleeding again. We're going to roll him on the comforter and drag the blanket over to the fireplace. I'll need your help; he's a big man."

She grabbed him by his belt at the waist and his right shoulder, then lifted while Ben stuffed the comforter underneath his body with plenty of room above his head. Out of breath, she said, "OK," and again she applied pressure to his shoulder to stop the bright red blood seeping through the cloth she'd used before. "Now go check Louna's pulse again before we do the other side."

"Shouldn't we call an ambulance, Mom?"

"I wish we could, sweetie, but there's no one to call."

When he returned from Louna's side, he said, "Same as before. Where's her brother, Andy?"

Maeve avoided her son's eyes. "I don't know, son. Help me with Bishop now."

This time, she reached over Bishop and pulled upward while Ben pulled the comforter through to the other side.

Again, she had to take time to stop the bleeding before she continued. At least now she could move him away from the front door, which was starting to look like a gory crime scene.

Together, both she and her son pulled and tugged the comforter with all their might and moved Bishop closer to the woodstove. That's when she really saw the extent of his condition. She had Ben hold the compress on his shoulder while she checked on Louna again. Her breath was shallow, but she was alive.

Quickly, Maeve ran to get antiseptic, scissors, tweezers, water, and clean washcloths. She began with the child and cut away her nightgown while Ben hid his eyes. She started at the top of the child and washed away as much of the soot as possible and tweezed out all the glass she could find embedded in her skin and washed her again. Though she bled from cuts, there were no major gashes. Maeve applied antiseptic and then elevated her chest with pillows until she was almost sitting up; since her lungs were probably the biggest concern, removing as much weight from her chest as possible would be the best thing. Then she covered the girl with a fresh blanket and hoped for the best.

Then she moved to Bishop and again Ben helped her by removing his hat, coat, and gloves. Then she unbuckled his belt while Ben removed his socks. "What are we doing this for?" Ben asked.

"I need to see if he has any other injuries that we need to treat."

She cut away his thermal T-shirt with scissors to get to his damaged arm when Ben asked, "Won't he be mad?"

She shook her head. "No, he'll be thankful we helped him. Oh my," she said. "Look at that one." A large glass shard stabbed into his forearm.

"Ugh, he's going to need stitches, Mom."

"Yeah…" she said, and the realization dawned on her that she would have to be the one to do the stitching. She went to her home library and pulled out a first aid book and flipped through the pages. Nothing said what to do in case of a gunshot to the shoulder, but there were directions on how to stitch up a wound.

Again, she started at the top and washed away the grime. When she got to the large shard of glass in the back of his forearm, she waited until she'd removed all the other smaller ones because she knew this one would bleed a lot as soon as she took it out.

All along his chest she found embedded pieces of glass, and when she wiped away the blood, they pooled up again like little reservoirs. Applying a cold compress, she then waited for the bleeding to abate before dabbing on the antiseptic. Had he been awake she was sure he would have yelled out at the stinging pain, but then again, after she looked at the tough guy, perhaps not. He wasn't the complaining type, especially since he was more concerned about the girl than himself when he'd arrived.

"Ben, all the doors are locked, right?"

"Yes! I made sure."

With everything else going on, she couldn't shake the sounds from earlier and the thought that perhaps someone might come to the house after the shooting. *They had to have seen Bishop's tracks in the snow, right? Should I be concerned?*

"OK, come and sit with them while I get a few things together," she said instead of "while I find a needle and thread." While up, she peeked out the front window. The glow from the house fire down the road seemed to dim. Just in case, she checked the locks again and then checked the back door as well. After she had found the needle and thread in her sewing kit, she lit a lighter and slid the needle through the flame a few times and then wiped it down with alcohol. She'd never done this before and barely knew how to sew. The gash in Bishop's arm was around two inches long, and the injury to his shoulder was even bigger, but it had to be closed, and she was the only one here to do the stitching.

Preparing herself, she took a deep breath, then brought the supplies along with a few more clean towels back to her patient and knelt down next to him. "Ben, keep a watch on Louna. Tell me if anything changes."

"OK. I will," he said as he watched over Louna.

Just as she suspected, after pulling out the jagged glass shard from the back of his forearm the wound bled profusely. She made sure to remove all of the glass before she applied pressure. The wound gaped open, and there was no way around it—she had to sew it back together to join the edges.

After threading the needle by the light of the woodstove, she set to work. The first pull through the skin made her stomach roll. Maeve nearly lost it but pulled herself together, wiped away the blood, and stitched through the layers of skin.

Afterward, she covered the wound in antibacterial ointment and wrapped a bandage around the entire arm. Then she stood and went to wash her hands. Turning back to Bishop and talking to herself with her hands on her hips, she said, "I don't know what to do about the shoulder."

"Doesn't it say in the book?" Ben asked.

"No, I guess they figured in the case of a gunshot wound you'd go to the hospital."

"Mom, she's moving!" Ben yelled from beside Louna.

Maeve ran over to the couch and found the little girl stirring. "Ben, get a glass of water for her."

He ran to the kitchen while Maeve felt the girl's forehead. So far, there was no sign of fever in either patient, but she figured if there was a chance, it would happen. Ben returned with the water, and Maeve said, "Louna, you're all right. Can you hear me?"

The little girl moved her hand to her throat, and her eyelids fluttered. "She's trying to wake up," Ben said.

Maeve sat her up and held the cup to her mouth. A little of the water trickled past her small red lips, and a tiny stream spilled down the side of her cheek.

"Is she going to die, Mom?"

She had to tell him the truth. "I don't know, Ben. Not if I can help it."

She laid the girl's head back down on the pillow and checked for a pulse again. Knowing her lungs and esophagus were probably damaged from the hot air of the burning house, there was quite a good chance the girl would die.

"She's not going to die," came a gravelly voice from the pallet on the floor.

"Bishop! You're awake," Ben said.

Bishop tried to sit up and recoiled from the pain in his shoulder.

"Don't try to move!" Maeve said. "You've been shot through the shoulder."

He suddenly looked frantic. His eyes were wildly searching the room. "Where's my rifle?"

"Right here," Ben said, pointing to it on the chair next to him.

"Door's locked?"

"Yes, sir," Ben said, nodding his head.

"How's the girl?"

Maeve didn't know what to say. "She's breathing but still unconscious."

He struggled to sit up a little more, and Maeve helped him. He looked at his right shoulder. "Did the bullet go through?"

"There's an exit wound."

"Good, but we're going to need antibiotics. Do you have any in the house?"

She shook her head no. "It's illegal now to keep old medications."

Bishop nodded. "We can't stay here. Whoever that was who looted that house, they're organized. The others probably already found them, and there are clear tracks to this house through the snow. We have to leave before daylight."

He said just what she had feared before. "We can't leave. Where will we go?" Maeve nearly shouted. "It's freezing out there, and both you and this girl need medical attention. You can't travel."

"Where's my horse?"

"I put him in the garage," Ben said.

"So there are tracks in the snow outside everywhere? You're in danger here. We have to go now," he said and began to stand.

"Bishop, wait. Look at her," she said, pointing to the child. She was as white as the snow outside, drained of all color. "She could die out there. She needs rest."

"She'll die if we stay here, and so will you and Ben."

He looked around for his boots, and Ben brought them to him. He sat in a chair and began lacing them up as well as he could with the pain from the wound in his shoulder.

"Your wound. It's going to start bleeding again."

"Can you bring me a couple of spare T-shirts?"

She cursed under her breath but left the room in search of one of Roger's old T-shirts.

By the time she returned, Bishop already had his belt back on. He sucked in a sharp breath when he pushed the compress on his shoulder. A bright red stream of blood began to make a river down his bare chest.

"Take the first T-shirt and cut the seam open from the right sleeve all the way down to the hem."

She grabbed the scissors that she used to cut his thermal tee off of him earlier.

He nodded when she was done and reached for the shirt. She didn't give it to him, though. She knew he'd need help getting the shirt on while holding the compress with his left hand over his right shoulder.

"I can do it," he said, watching her as she approached him.

She shook her head and ignored him while she slipped the opening over his head. "You need help, Bishop." She opened the armhole and helped him slide his right hand through the opening.

"Now, pull the shirt taut and tie it high under my left arm with the cut ends," he said, somewhat reluctantly.

She wasn't sure if he just didn't like people touching him or if he didn't like her touching him. It didn't matter to Maeve, though. He needed help, and she was the only one who could help him now.

"Tighter," he said as she pulled the excess material taut under his left arm. She pulled harder, and when she did he sucked in another sharp breath out of pain.

"I'm sorry! Let's push a few more of those towels under there to put pressure on the wound."

He nodded with his lips pursed in a straight line. She hated to hurt him, but it must be done.

When they were through, she helped him put another T-shirt over the first and then his coat over that. Thankfully, he still had use of both arms.

"That'll do," Bishop said and tested out his right arm to see what his range of motion was. "Bundle the girl up and Ben too. We need to get to Jax. He'll know how to help the girl, and he has all the illegal antibiotics one could ask for."

"Who's Jax?"

Bishop stuck his knife into the holster on his belt and grabbed his AR-15 to sling over his back. His M9 Beretta, he replaced into its holster. Going to the front of the house, he looked out into the pitch-dark night. "*He's* a hermit," Bishop said and flashed a rare smile.

"Wait, Bishop. I don't know if I can trust you. I don't want to leave my home and take my son out into the forest in this terrible cold. What if no one comes here?"

Bishop looked at Ben, who was watching the two of them discuss things. She knew she shouldn't express her concerns like this in front of her son, but there was no other choice now.

"Take a good look at your boy. He's alive now. He won't be by sunup. Roger asked me to take care of you two when he was gone. You're not going to stop me from doing that."

Maeve took a step away from him. "What is that supposed to mean? We don't even know you."

"Your husband knew me, and he trusted me, and I'm going to keep my promise to him. Ben, get your gear on."

Her son scrambled for his coat and boots. She'd never seen him move so fast. In a way, she felt betrayed by her own son.

Then, when she looked back to Bishop, she found his stare burrowing into her. In a calm but stern voice, he said, "*Get* your coat on, Maeve."

A chill went up her spine. With only those five words he'd said volumes. She didn't ask what he'd do *if* she refused. She'd moved to the closet and put on her coat and stepped into her boots when she heard a noise in front of the house.

Bishop looked out the front and saw headlights down the road the way he'd come earlier, and someone yelled. Then there were shots fired.

"Move, now!" Bishop bellowed, and Maeve picked up the girl, who was wrapped only in blankets, while Bishop herded them into the garage.

From there, he didn't waste time. He pulled his horse out through the side door into the backyard and took the child while Maeve mounted the saddle. He handed the girl to her and swung Ben up behind his mother.

"Hold on to your mom," he said to Ben while the sounds of shots and men were gaining on the house.

He grabbed the horse's lead in one hand and held his Beretta in the other and ran to the tree line.

Maeve held on to the pommel while holding the girl, and her son held on for dear life. She hadn't ridden a horse since childhood but didn't even think about that as she and these children were being spirited away from killers who were now in her driveway. The last thing she saw before the total dark of the forest took over was headlights in her front driveway, and she heard the sound of her front window shattering in a volley of gunshots.

Chapter 14

Terrified by the loud gunfire, Ben had begun to weep as he clenched his mother's waist, his head buried in her back.

"Keep quiet," Bishop whispered to them as he led Jake through the dark woods. "And keep your heads down." He pulled them along and continuously surveyed their surroundings. They were nearly a mile northwest through the woods before Bishop broke his breakneck pace, though he still kept his guard up. *If I keep this up, I'm going to pass out, and that's not going to help them.* Before long, they made it to a ridge, and what he saw when he looked down angered him even more. "Maeve, look," he told her and pointed down into the darkness where not only was the original house smoldering, but her own house was up in flames as well as the neighbor's to the south of hers.

"Oh my God!" she yelled and tried to dismount the horse.

"No, stay there. There's nothing we can do."

He pulled them away from the scene and deeper into the forest while trying to ignore the searing pain in his shoulder. She wept quietly from time to time after walking another few hours. By then, Bishop knew Jake needed to rest. The light haze from the sun was beginning to creep over the mountains in the east, though they were within the forest's cocoon and could only see a dim brightness between the trees. They'd finally made it to their destination when they reached a slight clearing. Had he not known there was a resident here, he would have walked right past; only a trained eye could have seen the few signs of human habitation there.

"Why are we stopping?" Maeve asked. She was shivering in the cold, and at some point it had started snowing again. The red hair peeking out from underneath her knit hat was no longer auburn but white and crystallized. She'd barely put on her coat and boots before they'd fled the house, and the girl was only wrapped in blankets. He needed to get them into warm shelter quickly.

"We're here," he said, and when he looked up to the sky, so did she, and snowflakes cascaded down upon them.

"Bishop? That you?" an old voice asked.

Bishop pulled his rifle from around his back. Maeve's eyes widened. He put a finger to his mouth. "Yes," he said, without knowing where the voice was coming from. "I'm injured and so is a child. We need your help, Jax," he said as his eyes scanned the winter world around him.

"You know better than to bring strangers here," Jax bellowed.

"I had no choice, Jax. We'll be on our way as soon as you help us."

"No," Jax said. "Take them away!" His loud voice echoed through space as Maeve jumped and trembled in the saddle.

"We're staying until you help us, Jax. There's a little girl here. She'll die if you don't. She was in a house fire, Jax."

His words were met with silence…at first.

"They're all going to die," the disembodied voice rang out. Bishop shifted his weight and spun to the right, his rifle out in front, ready.

"Please!" Maeve screamed and flung her head up, the snow scattering away and revealing her red locks. "She's not breathing, Bishop. She stopped breathing!"

Bishop pulled Maeve from the saddle along with the child in her arms. They laid her out on the snow. Her bloodstained blond hair cascaded about her. She lay like a tiny angel. Her lips were blue as Bishop arched her small neck and began to breathe life into her torn lungs. Maeve cried on her knees as Ben sat atop Jake looking on at the futile scene before him.

After chest compressions and blowing air into the girl, she began to breathe on her own again. Bishop cradled her.

"Oh, thank God!" Maeve exclaimed.

Standing with the girl in his left arm, he lifted his rifle with his injured right arm.

"Jax! Enough, get down—" was all he had uttered before he saw three black lengths of cloth floating to the ground from above.

"What are those?" Maeve asked.

Bishop blew out a breath. "Blindfolds."

Chapter 15

Holding onto her son, Maeve clenched each time she detected someone brushing up against her. The man known as Jax was not friendly in the least.

"All I ask is that people leave…me…*alone!*" he hollered, and then there was silence for a time.

"The child's dying, Jax. The town has lost control. Looters are taking what they want and killing anyone they run across."

"So? That's not my problem!"

She had no idea what was going on. Bishop whispered to her that everything would be all right as he tied the blindfold over her eyes. She couldn't see a thing and neither could the girl if she were conscious or her son who sat next to her. She had no idea where they were. All she knew was one minute Bishop was leading them in the snow by the hand as she held onto Ben outside in the freezing air, and the next minute they walked into a narrow passageway and the further they walked the warmer it became.

The sound of a fire crackled somewhere nearby. Her son curled into her side, and she guessed he was listening to everything around them as she was. Bishop was the only one without a blindfold, which told her he'd been here before and perhaps the man named Jax trusted him.

"She might not make it, Bishop. Her lungs, they're scorched."

"Do what you can, Jax."

The man brushed past her legs again. He was between her and the fire, and each time he passed she could feel that lack of heat emanating from the fire. There were clanking noises and the sounds of him crushing something, then a pungent smell of wintergreen.

"You're all right, Maeve. Don't worry. Here, drink this," Bishop said and touched her shoulder as he held something to her lips.

She swallowed a liquid that tasted like water but was tinged with something she didn't recognize.

"Rest while you can," he said, and Ben laid his head on her lap after Bishop gave him a sip too. She felt a fur blanket being wrapped around them both. "There's a pillow on your left—you can lie down."

Bishop nudged her in that direction, and she held Ben to her side as he helped her lie down.

She grabbed his wrist when she felt him nearby. "Are we safe here?" she whispered.

His breath caressed the side of her cheek when he said, "Yes. I won't let anything happen to you, Maeve. You'll have to trust me."

I have no choice, she thought as she drifted off to sleep.

Chapter 16

He didn't want to do it, but when Jax handed him the cup he'd just mixed and nodded to Maeve and her son, he knew it was a condition of their presence there. They would sleep while Jax worked on the girl and his shoulder. They needed the sleep anyway, especially since they were traumatized by the events that had happened earlier.

Jax was a complicated man. He was brilliant but disturbed and went for long periods without any human contact. He only tolerated a few of them, the ones in the woods, and Bishop was one of them.

He'd first discovered Jax while fishing early one morning. After fishing in one spot and coming up skunked, he was going to check out another area when he saw a barefoot man dressed in rags on a boulder, but it was what he was doing that caught Bishop's attention.

He was practicing what Bishop recognized as taekwondo with a little judo thrown in. His moves were clean and swift for a guy who looked to be in his sixties. The stranger was tall and thin and sported a long gray beard, but what struck Bishop most was the man's tormented eyes. He'd recognized the pain almost immediately because he knew without looking that he wore those same windows to the soul.

Bishop had begun to back away the way he'd come, but before he knew it, the stranger held a Kimber 1911 handgun on him and carefully scissored a few paces to pick up a Winchester rifle leaning against a tree with his other hand. The man apparently wasn't messing around.

"This is my place," he warned finally after staring at him long enough to study Bishop thoroughly. "Go find yourself another."

And he did. He hadn't seen even a sign of the strange man, and then he came down with a cold so strong he thought it must be pneumonia. Bishop thought himself a dead man and was happy at the prospect, to be honest, but during his delirium, he'd seen the man standing over him inside of his cave, forcing liquids into his mouth, nearly drowning him at times. Bishop never could figure out how the man knew that Bishop was sick or how he'd gained entry to his home.

Horrible smells of something the stranger was cooking over his stove permeated everything. He was torturing him, Bishop was sure of it. Somewhere in the nightmare, he'd asked him his name, and the stranger had given it to him as a gift. Then, suddenly, he was gone when Bishop's fever broke. He'd left him with a pungent liquid to drink and didn't set eyes on him again for another year after he'd recovered.

Since that time, they occasionally met in the woods, only speaking with few words. Bishop brought him meat from fresh kills but wasn't sure if that was payment enough for Jax having saved his life. Jax never seemed to appreciate it either way. He mostly wanted to be left alone, and Bishop understood.

Now, he depended on Jax to save the girl and himself. He was sure an infection would start in his shoulder soon, and he'd be worthless to Maeve and her son then.

There was much to do, too. None of this would get any better, and hiding in the woods was only a temporary solution. At the moment, they were hiding from the greatest threat—man—but soon the weather would trump man as the greatest danger.

He couldn't keep them here for the long term. The ice age would last for years, and the killers needed to be exterminated, or it was likely the whole town of Coeur d'Alene would succumb to the few who'd gained power in the crisis.

These things were easy to predict for a soldier of war, one who'd watched the worst of atrocities. Man's true nature, once all the façade of the modern-day world was stripped away, was nothing more than beast. To survive, man would smile at a mother and butcher her child to eat if he were starving—and save her for later. There was nothing man wouldn't do to ensure his own survival. "We're fickle like that," Jax once said to him. "We'll praise humanity as the height of honor but murder the likes of humans in any shape they come, give all for a meal, an unremitting quench."

The girl's lips were no longer blue. Her thin face was still devoid of color though Jax last said she might have a chance. Her breathing was raspy, and Jax kept a steam going around her that smelled of pine forest. He continually crushed dried berries he had inside of dark hide pouches and mixed them with other equally mystifying herbs into a poultice that he smeared with honey on the girl's chest. The stench was nearly unbearable. Then Jax made Bishop remove his shirt when the blood began seeping through.

Again Jax complained and moaned as he attacked several dried items in his mortar and pummeled them into a paste. This time, the stuff he applied looked like tar and smelled more like licorice than mint as he slathered a thick layer over both sides of Bishop's shoulder wound. Then Jax wrapped a large leaf over both sides before rewrapping his shoulder.

"It'll heal on its own. Leave that alone for a week. Drink this too." He handed him a cup of something foul, and Bishop grimaced before downing the entire thing.

"You're such a baby."

Bishop didn't bother with a comeback. "Thank—"

"Shut up." Jax cursed him as Bishop found himself falling over and onto the seat where Maeve and her son were sleeping.

Bastard, Bishop thought before he fell unconscious.

Chapter 17

Shadows passed against a flame. Her eyes mere slits, Maeve couldn't keep them open but for a brief moment, followed by another struggle to lift her eyelids.

Again she tried, and finally with all her strength they fluttered open but had all intentions of slamming shut again. Struggling with all her might and finally gaining the strength to keep them open, her eyes searched the room for Ben; a primal need to find him overtook her. She tried to move her arm, and again it was a monumental feat of effort just to raise one finger.

Whatever Bishop had given her to drink, the concoction had knocked her out, and now she was struggling to stay awake. The warmth from the fire was almost too much as she lay under a fur blanket, and the person next to her smelled awful. His skin sweated onto her shirt. She stirred and found that the hand she was trying to move was draped over his bare arm. The arm belonged to Bishop, and she recoiled away from him, realizing she was cuddled against his side in a way too intimate for a stranger.

Maeve pulled herself into a sitting position and out from the stifling heat of the blankets, finding Ben asleep on her other side.

She pushed on his shoulder. "Ben. Wake up." His small body jerked with her efforts. It didn't matter how much she jostled him, though; he didn't move on his own. His little chest rose with each breath, and she was consoled by the fact that he was merely sleeping. Then it dawned on her. *Where are the blindfolds?* she wondered and then looked around the room she found herself in. *This isn't the same place we were in before.* The room they were in before took stairs to climb. This place had a solid floor of stone and felt like a cellar or cave of some kind. In front of her, there was a fire pit made of stone. The flames blazed away at the logs inside, and beyond that, there was a locked wooden door with a cast-iron handle. They were lying on a pallet on top of a cold stone floor. "Where are we?"

Bishop's arm was wrapped in the half T-shirt with some horrible-smelling medicine underneath. Beyond him lay the girl next to his side.

"Louna," she called out and scrambled out from between the blankets. Maeve's shoes were off, and her socks caught on the rough stone floor. When she rounded the other side of the girl, she found her asleep but breathing well next to Bishop.

"Bishop must have moved us here," she reasoned, staring beyond the girl at the man sleeping. "How, I don't know."

She looked around the enclosed room and found the rest of their shoes and Bishop's firearms piled nearby. Closer to the door there was a bucket full of what she hoped was water. She took a metal mug from nearby and dipped the cup in the water and smelled it first before she dared take a sip. The water was crisp and cold and tasted pure. She quickly brought the mug to her son and lifted his head with her arm while holding the cup to his lips. "Ben, can you hear me? Take a sip."

He did and then no more. She laid him back down and checked him over. Satisfied that he was all right, she brought the cup to Louna, and though the girl did not respond she was able to get some of the liquid past her lips. Next, she went to Bishop and tried the same technique. "Bishop, wake up."

His eyes bolted open, and his response scared her so much she spilled the water down his chest. "I'm sorry," she said, and he looked at them in alarm.

"Where's Jax?"

"I...I don't know. I just woke up."

"Where are we?"

"I don't know. I thought you brought us here."

He shook his head. "No, I didn't." He looked at the sleeping girl at his side and checked her pulse. And then he looked to Ben.

"He's fine. He's still asleep."

"Where's Jake?" he said after he had realized both children slept on either side of him.

"Who's Jake?"

He looked at her with frustration. "The horse!"

"I don't know," she said, still holding the empty mug.

This was like some kind of bizarre dream that she was still trying to figure out.

When Bishop stood, he swayed a little and caught himself on the stone wall.

"Where are we?" she asked him.

"I...I think we're in one of Jax's hideouts. He must have brought us here."

"How did he do that? I thought you brought us here."

"He really doesn't like to be around people."

"Well, it's not OK for him to put us all to sleep and move us around like that," she yelled.

"Yeah, but we're alive, and the girl sounds good, too."

He pushed a few fingers to his wound. "I wonder how long we've been here," he said as he walked toward the wooden door.

"I have no idea," she said and realized she was still holding on to the metal mug. She set it down.

"Had to only be a day. He must keep coming to reload the fire pit."

Bishop slipped his feet into his boots and picked up his Beretta and pulled the iron lever on the door. Cold air and flurries blew inside. The fire protested and roared while Maeve pulled the fur blanket up over the children to shield them from the sudden cold.

His face reflected the whiteness outside until he shut the door again.

He confirmed her suspicion when he said, "Blizzard."

"Great. Now, what do we do?"

"Well, Jax will be back—I'd say in about two hours according to the fire. Unless he knew exactly what time we'd wake, which he probably did. And, in that case, he won't be back."

"We need to get into town. This girl needs real medical attention, and we need to let the authorities know what happened."

He shook his head. "She's going to be fine, and there's no town to go to. Those guys who robbed your neighbor and killed her parents...It's more than likely that same scenario is going on all around Coeur d'Alene as well as everywhere else. This is what happens to society when everything goes to hell. The evil prey on the clueless."

"What do you mean? This is just a national disaster. It'll blow over in a few days. The police will arrest the looters and then we can go home."

"Your home was burned to the ground, Maeve. Don't you remember that?"

She remembered then…the girl's home was smoldering, and her own house was ablaze with fire. "We can't just stay here."

He didn't say anything else for a while. The wood continued to snap and crack in the fireplace. "We'll need water, food, and…facilities," she said, trying to hint that she had to go.

"We'll go back to my place when the snow dies down."

"Where's your horse?"

"He's out there under an overhang. Jax wouldn't harm Jake or us. He just doesn't like to interact with people."

She nodded but still didn't think it was an excuse for him to put everyone to sleep for his own comfort level.

Ben began to stir then. He rubbed his eyes and sat up. "Where are we?"

She shook her head. "I have no idea, but we're safe."

"Is Louna OK?" Ben asked.

"We think so. Her breathing sounds better."

An hour later, when the fire died down, they gathered their belongings and Bishop wrapped the girl in the fur hide. Again, Bishop helped Maeve up onto Jake, and he handed the unconscious child to her. She smelled like winter berries, and Maeve wished Jax was a little friendlier so that he'd share some of his secrets with her because she had no idea how he'd made the child's near-death condition improve to merely resting. As peaceful as she was in sleep with her long, dark lashes against her alabaster skin, her world would shatter when she woke. So as long as she could sleep, Maeve wanted her to, just to keep her life peaceful for a little while longer.

The sun, dim as it was through the pouring snow, seemed to be behind the gray sky to the west. She figured it must be about two in the afternoon as they slogged through the cold. She worried about Bishop. He was frozen through, and snow clung to his hat and coat so thickly that he looked miserable. Bishop led them through the forest and finally stopped near a stack of boulders that she would have never noticed were a home unless Bishop had pointed it out. He opened a gate after swiping his thumb on a black pad and then took the bundle from her lap after helping Ben down from the horse. Snow that had accumulated on them dropped to the ground or froze in place on her hat and in her hair.

They went inside the cave past a kitchen and then deeper into a large stone room filled with bunks and a lot of boxes. It reminded her of a hobbit hole, but she'd never say that out loud in his presence.

Everything was perfectly laid out in straight lines. She could recognize an engineering man anywhere. Her father was one and wouldn't condone curves or angles in home décor. The beds were in even rows. The utensils were laid out in lines and perfectly straight on his table. There were no extras or flourishes.

"You live here?" Ben asked Bishop.

"Yes," Bishop said and handed the girl back to Maeve and averted his eyes while he cleared his throat.

"I'll put Jake away and be back in a minute." His eyes looked at her warily. She wasn't certain he trusted her in his home. After all, he was only a few hundred steps away from Jax. They were both hermits in their own pain living out in the woods. The comparisons were likely drawn.

She laid Louna out on one of the cots and checked her breathing again. It was as normal as Ben's was when sleeping. She removed the snow-covered blanket and covered her with another blanket that was lying on the end of one of the cots. Then Bishop returned and stared at her like she'd been up to something.

"I swear I haven't touched anything," she said to him.

"It's OK. There's nothing you can harm here."

"Look, I have a bookstore downtown. Ben and I can stay there. You don't have to keep us here."

"I doubt your bookstore is still standing, Maeve, and if it is, it's not safe." He began removing his gear and then gathered a few utensils and a few bottles of water. She sat next to her son on a cot that leaned against a boulder as he started a fire in the woodstove. "I don't mean to discourage you, Maeve. In a day or two, I'll scout down there and see what's going on. For now, we stay here," he said.

"I'm starving," Ben said, and so was she.

Bishop took three caramel-brown pouches out of a nearby box and tore the tops off of each one. After reshaping them, each pouch stood on its own while he poured boiling water into each one.

"Something smells good," Ben said as they watched steam rise from the bags.

Bishop handed them each a packet.

"What is it?" Ben asked.

"Chicken a la King, according to the package label, but it could be anything."

Ben was right. She was starving too, and when she took a bite of the brown bag's contents, it tasted like mushy chicken bouillon, and it was wonderful. She began to look at the contents and poked around with her fork. There were green peas in there, but the rest looked like reconstituted rice and chicken pieces.

"I wouldn't dissect it if I were you. Less appetizing that way," Bishop said, and she smiled.

He was probably right. So Maeve blindly scooped up spoonfuls into her mouth and swallowed.

After she was through, she handed him the empty packet, and then he tossed them into the fire. She watched while the package shrank and sizzled. *What am I going to do now? My home and all I've worked for is gone.*

Chapter 18

Later that night, Maeve tucked Ben into a nearby cot next to Louna. The girl still slept. She checked over her many cuts and abrasions for any sign of infection but found nothing alarming. Whatever Jax had put on them was healing them well.

"Bishop, do you have a spare T-shirt or something we can put on Louna? When she wakes, she might be startled to find she's undressed."

He'd been staring at the fire too, lost in his own world, when she began to talk to him. He rose from his seat on a spare log. "Sure," he said and rummaged around in the boxes. He handed her a grayish-white T-shirt that once was bright white but was now at least clean.

She slipped the crewneck over the girl's head and pulled each arm through the too-large shirt and then slipped it down past her torso, the hem nearly reaching her knees. She covered the child again and wiped Louna's hair out of her eyes after slipping a little more water between her lips. The only thing to do now was wait for her to wake up. There was nothing else she could think to do.

Perhaps she had relatives nearby who would take her. Maeve had only met the family down the road a few times. Anyone that lived out in the woods did so for a reason. Her reason was Roger and his need for peace. They weren't hermits, not like Bishop and Jax, but they hadn't wanted and didn't need a lot of excitement in their lives while raising their son.

"Mom, when are we going home?" Ben asked sleepily.

"Well, I'm not sure. The snow is piling high out there. It might be a few days, but this is like camping out, don't you think?" She didn't want to tell him the truth. She wasn't sure of the truth herself.

"Did those bad guys burn down our house too?"

She had no idea what was left of their house or how much Ben saw from the ridge that night Bishop led them to safety. She'd thought her son was asleep on the back of the horse with her.

Smiling, she pulled the blanket higher under his chin. "I don't know, Ben, but if they did, we'll find something else. Don't worry."

Her attention turned to the door as Bishop stepped outside. She wondered where he was going. She tucked her son in and made sure he and Louna were warm enough. The cave was an ingenious shelter, but it was drafty and cold, so a fire was always needed to keep them from freezing.

"Maeve," Bishop called suddenly when he opened the door a crack.

"What?"

"Put your coat on and come out here for a minute. I need to show you something."

She looked over the children again, making doubly sure they were both warm enough, and went back from the cave entrance to the cabin addition and put on her coat and boots and gloves again. They were still damp from the day before, but there was no other option. She stepped out into the night quickly and shut the door behind her. He stood nearby. The moon glowed eerily through the clouds.

"Come here," he whispered. "You have to see this."

She stepped toward him, and he took her by the arm and led her into the woods.

"I don't want to leave the children."

"We're not going far."

He led her up to a rocky ledge where they could see the valley below. What she expected were a few home fires like before if the looters were still out. What she saw was devastating. Down below, the town of Coeur d'Alene looked as if it had been bombed by warplanes. Even from that far away there were shouts she could hear and sirens or alarms that wouldn't soon fade. The whole town looked like it was on fire, and even the lake had burning boats lingering listlessly, smoke mixing with the night. Gunshots rang out in the distance as if war had been declared.

"This is what I meant," he said. "Strip away humanity in its modern form and only savagery remains."

She looked at his profile. The glow from the fires below reflected in his eyes. This man had seen war alongside her dead husband.

"We have to do something!" she said.

He shook his head. "No. I'm not doing anything to endanger you and the children in there."

She pointed toward the blaze. "There are more people down there who need your help, Bishop."

"I swore to protect you and Ben. That's all. If I go down there right now, there's a good chance you and Ben will die. After three days, I'll go down. I'll go down there and see what remains and what I can do, but for now, we wait and watch."

"It's all gone, isn't it?" She began to cry for all the children down there. For all of her friends, the teachers, the entire town who had harbored her in the worst of her grief.

Without thinking, he put a hand on her back and then pulled it away.

She turned to him, surprised.

"Yes. It's all gone from us now. Here and everywhere else. Let's get back. There will be more people fleeing into the woods now trying to get away. We need to keep watch."

He led her back inside the shelter and locked the door. She'd noticed he was always armed, always listening, and always aware of his surroundings. She supposed it was a habit that was hard to break after what he'd been through. Roger had said once that it was hard to turn off, and some veterans never did. She knew that he'd meant Bishop now.

"Go to sleep, Maeve. I'll wake you in a few hours to take the next watch."

He looked exhausted by the firelight, and though she thought it might be better if she took watch first, she didn't argue with him. She slipped into the cot next to the children's, afraid the images from the past day would haunt her and keep her awake, but instead, she fell fast asleep. It was as if her mind couldn't cope and switched off her consciousness like a light.

Chapter 19

"Maeve, wake up."

At first, she didn't know where she was. Then she heard a child crying.

"I don't know what to do with her. She needs you."

Someone jostled her arm again when she began to drift off. "OK, I'm coming," she said, and the girl's crying became louder.

When she sat up, she found Bishop kneeling in the cave room next to the girl, who was huddled on a chair by the fire. "It's OK. Maeve will be here soon. She'll help you. No one's going to hurt you," he was saying to her.

"Louna!" Maeve finally said when she realized what was going on.

Bishop turned to her. He had a hold of his rifle and looked at her seriously. "Can't you take over now and keep her quiet?"

She nodded. Something told her more was going on than the girl making noise.

"Hi, Louna. Do you remember me? I'm Ben's mom. We live down the road from you."

The girl made no signs of recognition. She had her knees drawn up to her chest under the T-shirt with a blanket wrapped around herself. She shook her head and appeared thoroughly frightened. Maeve tucked the blanket around her exposed feet. "No one's going to hurt you here. OK?" she said and ran her hand over the girl's hair.

When Louna tried to talk, her voice came out ragged. "Where's my…mom?" she said, and large tears pooled in her eyes. Suspecting the tears were coming from pain as well as fear, Maeve did her best to soothe the girl.

The child of only five years was utterly confused, and for good reason. Maeve wasn't certain five-year-olds could understand their conditions. "Sweetheart, there was a fire. Do you remember anything?"

She shook her head no.

Maeve didn't know where to begin. "There was a fire at your house, and the man from earlier saved you. He brought you to me. I live down the road from you. Ben is my son. Do you remember Ben?"

A flicker of recognition appeared in her eyes, but she cried still. The only thing Maeve could do was hold her and let the tears fall.

Bishop stuck his head in the door. "Can you keep her quiet? There's movement out here."

Maeve picked her up and took her back into the cave, farther from the door. "Louna, please try to be quiet for me, sweetheart," she whispered.

Louna buried her face into Maeve's neck and held on to her as if someone were trying to pry her away. Soon her sobs quieted, and when Maeve checked, the girl had fallen asleep.

The door to the cabin opened an hour later, and Maeve was still sitting against the cave wall with Louna clutched to her chest.

Bishop's shadow lingered on the pavement, stretching into the cave room before he entered. "She OK?"

Maeve nodded, though she wasn't sure any of them were OK. "What was going on out there?"

"Some people, a family I suspect, were roaming through the woods. They had backpacks. I didn't want to confront them if they went around our camp here. I kept an eye on them until they were clear through to the south. I don't know where they think they are headed—there's nothing that way, and they'll probably try to backtrack in a few days when they realize their mistake. I suspect we'll see a lot more people roaming through these woods soon."

"Why not help them?"

"Maeve, you see these boxes?"

She looked at the far wall where there were at least thirty large containers. "Those are filled with what you had for dinner. In another two days, people will kill for what's in those boxes."

She wasn't sure she believed him. "There's food down there in the stores. There are ranchers and farmers nearby."

"Maeve, this snow that's falling isn't going away for a long time. We'll be digging ourselves out of this for years. It's not going to end or blow over, and there will be no spring. There will be no harvest next year or any year for a long time to come because this isn't going to end."

She looked at the boxes again. "We don't have enough here then, if what you say is true."

"Now you're beginning to grasp our situation."

She stared at him awhile longer. She couldn't make out his features as he stood in the doorway, the fireplace shadowing his features. "Is it my turn to take the watch?"

"I let you sleep through the night. It's daytime, Maeve."

She couldn't believe it. It was still dark as ebony outside. "What time is it?"

"Nine in the morning," he said.

She laid Louna down on the cot carefully in order not to wake her and then walked past Bishop. He stood to the side as she slipped by him. She peeked out into the darkness. "It can't be nine a.m. It's pitch dark out there."

"It hasn't stopped snowing all night." He looked at his watch and again said definitely, "Nine in the morning."

"Still, I've never seen it so dark at this time. Why didn't you wake me?"

"Because the hikers were coming through. I doubt there will be many now, though. I'll try to sleep a few hours if you can keep watch now."

"I will," she said and pulled the Glock out from her coat pocket.

"Is that still loaded?"

"Yes."

"When's the last time you shot it?"

"I don't know. Two, three years ago?"

"If you hear something, yell at me first before you do anything. Just sit right here," he said, pointing to the chair by the door. "Don't move from this chair unless you hear something, and wake me before you act. Understand?"

She nodded again.

He started to walk toward the cave room.

"What if it's just people walking by?"

"If you hear any noise out of the ordinary, wake me. Even if it's just people walking through."

His voice was gruff and lacked patience. She decided not to ask any further questions.

She heard him settle on the cot closest to the doorway, and when she glanced over, he had one boot on the ground. She had no idea how he was going to sleep like that, but she wasn't going to say anything. Instead, as his snores became louder and the children still slept, she sat there gazing out into the darkness for any signs of danger.

Chapter 20

Over the next few days, Maeve looked after the children as Bishop scouted their camp day and night, watching as refugees from the town below sought safer havens in the wilderness. He never confronted the people he detected in the forest unless they were at risk of finding their hidden camp. If they strayed too close, he would intervene, sending a few warning shots to encourage their circumvention of the area.

Why they couldn't help at least those families with children was something Maeve didn't understand. They'd argued about the dilemma. "If we help more, that means one of those two kids in there will die of starvation one day sooner. You choose which one," he'd said. She couldn't, of course, and that was the end of their debate over helping strangers.

Louna and Ben played quietly in the bunk room most of the time, but she sensed a restlessness in Bishop when there was too much noise going on. He would often leave the cabin without saying where he was going, returning empty handed. She encouraged the children to play quietly and tried to refrain from asking him too many questions in an attempt to help ease the man into having them there. After watching the town below from the view on the cliff, she too was shocked at all the violence she'd seen and heard. There was no going back home like this; she'd never want to endanger Ben or Louna, so she trusted Bishop's plan to wait.

On the third morning, she woke to find Bishop cleaning and then loading his weapons near the light of the woodstove. Without a shirt on, she could see his shoulder injury still seeped blood through the bandage. Though he rarely mentioned the wound, she knew he must still be in a lot of pain. Her eyes lingered over Bishop's chest as he placed extra boxes of ammunition carefully in a pack along with a few MREs, a bundle of rope, and a first aid kit among other items. "Where are you going?" she said in a soft voice.

"Down there. I told you, we'd wait for the first die off and then I'd go down and see what's going on. From my observations, there's organized looting and executions. Nothing good is happening. I'm going to go down and find out who's in charge." He said as he put on a shirt and then his outwear and then slung the pack over his shoulder. "I'll be back tonight."

"Wait!" Terrified, Maeve got up and chased him to the front door. Scared that he might be leaving her and the children for good, she tried to stall him. "You're not leaving-leaving us, right? I know you're not used to being around people, but I promise we'll try to stay quiet."

"Maeve…"

"Seriously, Bishop, I…can't keep watch and protect us the way that you do. I'm scared," she whispered loudly, trying to keep her voice down with the children nearby.

He put his hand on her shoulder as she stared into his blue eyes.

"I'm not leaving you. I'd never do that. I swear I'm only going down to recon the area—get as much information as I can about what's going on down there. In the meantime, do what I showed you. Keep the door locked and keep watch. If you detect anyone, hide unless confronted, and then you know what to do. Maybe you and the kids could also stuff the cracks in the walls with paper or whatever you can find to help keep the draft out. When the kids have to go out, take them to the same area as before and hurry them back. It's snowing again, so there's more cover."

"When has it ever stopped in the last three days?" she asked.

"A few hours last night," he whispered. "You'll be fine. I'll be back soon after dark."

She nodded, and he squeezed her shoulder.

"Fear is good, Maeve. It'll help you survive."

She wasn't just afraid—she was terrified. But Maeve gave him a brave smile, and when he stepped out into the snow, she locked the latch and watched him through the cracks and fallen snow as he saddled Jake and left her and the children there in the cabin alone.

Chapter 21

Bishop set out to scout the town of Coeur d'Alene, which meant he'd have to cross the lake at some point. The pitch-black darkness had lightened to a stone gray. He was betting that by now the weather had frozen the first eight inches of the lake water as it does during hard winters at the end of January.

To the north of the highway was all urban sprawl. To the south stood the main town: lots of shops, residential areas, and one enormous luxury fifteen-floor resort hotel attached to a marina and a world-class golf course on the shores of Lake Coeur d'Alene.

The building itself stood as a hallmark over the lake for which the town was named. One family owned the hotel as well as many of the surrounding businesses, and if it weren't for that family Coeur d'Alene would not likely be the gem of the town that it was. Of course, the beauty of the area was the major draw in the summer months, and in the frigid months, when the lake froze over, Coeur d'Alene became a winter wonderland.

Bishop had visited the resort on occasion as a child, once for a wedding and another time for his parent's anniversary dinner, where on the top floor he'd gazed out at twilight as the entire lake reflected a crimson sunset. There were few more beautiful sights in the world. Of course, those were only memories from a time before the war.

He'd once heard his father describe the family who owned the place as being hardworking and generous. Those were attributes his father seldom used, so Bishop always held high regard for them. What had happened to the family now was a mystery. All he could glean from his spot on the mountain above and from the other south of the lake was that something had gone terribly wrong. Fires burned continuously, and there were occasional explosions. The lake itself held hostage a number of burned boats, now surrounded by a thick layer of ice. Gunshots rang out and echoed through the thin winter air with the sound echoing far. And dark smoke mixed and mingled with the already gray skies.

The sounds of constant shooting only began to recede in the coming day. Bishop had guessed a three-day waiting period would likely tell him more. He couldn't bring Maeve and the children down in these conditions, and he couldn't keep her up there with the way the weather was going. Something had to give. Their rations wouldn't hold out forever, and he needed to find a safer place for Maeve and the children for the long term.

He rode Jake down through the forest, stopping every now and then and using his binoculars to scan the area before him for people in the woods. That's when he heard a yell for help and, leery of approaching any stranger, he kept his distance. But he was too close to whoever was causing the distraction, and he was afraid that someone else might come and spot him, so he tethered Jake nearby and scouted closer to the person who was urgently calling out.

While walking through the snow, he saw many individual tracks, and a lot of the snowy prints were laced with blood. There was little other noise in the forest. An eerie calm had taken over since the weather turned. Dark gray skies were the new normal, and when he finally peered around a frozen ravine, he saw why the guy was calling out. Though the man could not see him, he could see the ashen hiker yelling with his femur puncturing through the skin of his leg and canvas pants. He was overweight and must have stumbled over the uneven terrain under the snow. You had to know these woods well enough to remember where obstacles hid underneath.

Not only was the guy's leg broken, but he was also bleeding from the chest. There was no way he would survive. Not in these present conditions. Bishop was about to move on, but perhaps he might be able to get a little information from the man. He went back to Jake and pulled his water thermos out offering the bottle to the man dying in the snow.

The man had called out a few more times since he'd spied him, and besides information Bishop also wanted the man to stop screaming and drawing attention to the area leading up to his hideout. More people would come along this path and possibly follow his tracks.

Bishop hiked back quickly to the man and revealed himself over the ledge of the narrow ravine between the trees, letting the near-dead man see him.

"Hello there," he said.

The man's pudgy face was startled for a second, not believing someone had actually come in answer to his calls.

"Hey, hey, I've hurt my leg. I think I broke my leg."

He wore a black-and-red scotch flannel jacket over jeans and a T-shirt. His large hands were blue from the cold. His big fingers stuck out at right angles from his hand like an opened glove. There was no way he could move them. Bishop thought they were probably frozen through. His goatee was ice crusted, but oddly enough he didn't even shiver though he was stuck there in the snow and had been for a long time. He was a dead man, only he didn't know it yet.

"Looks like you're bleeding there, too. What happened to you?"

"Shot…" he said, bewildered.

Bishop thought the guy was probably in shock. His speech was slurred, and he looked as if he was hallucinating.

"*Who* shot you?" Bishop asked him while he carefully climbed down the ravine.

"Those guys…security guys from the hotel, they're taking everything. Said…they were running things now."

"Where are the police? Who's the leader?" Bishop asked while he opened the thermos. The stranger eyeballed the container.

"I don't know. Can you help me? My leg's broken."

He was repeating himself. Bishop gave him a tight smile. "Can you take a sip of water for me?"

He nodded, and Bishop held the thermos to his blue lips. He eagerly drank down the liquid.

"Do you have family down there?"

"They shot them," he said as he wiped his mouth with the back of his right forearm. Bishop could see his fingers were thoroughly frostbitten, so blue they were black at the tips. He wouldn't last but a few more hours at the most. Even if he managed to get him to a modern medical facility, the guy was doomed.

The man started to lay his head down, and Bishop knew it wouldn't be long before he died. "Hey, what's your name?" Bishop asked as he patted the dead man on the shoulder.

"I'm Michael…Mike…I'm Mike…" He seemed to struggle for his last name. The cold did terrible things to the human brain. With his eyes staring straight up, his head slumped to the side.

"That's all right, Mike. Go to sleep," Bishop whispered and closed the man's wide-open eyes.

Bishop examined Mike's body. He had no weapons on him. He wore clothes typical for strolling the dry streets of the city below but not for slogging through the backcountry where he was now. No, Mike had run from something, and the blast through his shoulder had come from the back with the bullet exiting through the front. It wasn't the broken leg or the gunshot that killed him, though; it was the cold. Although these residents lived in a typically hard winter area, they didn't *live* in the cold, and Bishop suspected there would be many more deaths coming in the following weeks.

Bishop pushed layers of snow over Mike's body. It was the least he could do for the man. He'd given him information, but unfortunately, he was as good as dead when he found him. There was someone down there making life much more difficult in these tough times, and after Bishop found out who that was he would make a plan from there.

After retrieving Jake, he continued down to the lake and crossed Albion Road. The snow had piled in drifts in the opened areas between the trees. The wind picked up and made traversing the terrain even more challenging, and yet there was no end in sight.

He came to a stop near an old pier, looking out cautiously in the open. To his left, the lake widened substantially toward the marina. Gray skies coupled with the snow and thick gray smoke from fires made the area on the ice look like a war zone. He heard more sporadic shooting, but the smog was so thick in that area he couldn't make out anything.

The ice looked thick enough to traverse, but those were the famous last thoughts of many dead individuals. A small fishing boat stood captured in the center, the ice so thick it piled up around the hull as it expanded.

When Bishop typically crossed the lake, he took the beat-up metal rowboat he kept tied to the pier, but it had sunk and half frozen into the ice under the pier. This was the narrow end of the lake, and unless he crossed here, he'd have to circle the lake and follow the highway down to the town, which would add hours to his trek. He shifted in his saddle, looking all around him. This place, once peaceful, now seemed haunted.

Bishop dismounted and took a few steps. The ice was rough, and there were a few human tracks in areas. "Come on, Jake," he said and nudged the horse out onto the ice. He watched for any fissures as he went.

Crossing the lake in November was never done. Not in his lifetime, and he was sure it hadn't happened since the last Maunder Minimum in this area. Midway through, they passed the boat frozen in time. There was no one aboard, though Bishop didn't look deep inside. The faint tracks on the ice showed that someone else had checked out the boat and continued on to the other side.

Constantly vigilant of cracking ice, Bishop kept moving and led Jake behind him, never standing in one spot longer than the time it took to take the next step. Continuously transferring his and Jake's weight kept them from gambling against the ice's strength.

They reached the other side of the lake, and Bishop remounted while keeping watch for any other living person. Desperation hung heavy in the frozen air, and with the occasional shots ringing out in the distance he didn't think it would be long before he saw much worse than human desperation. Human despair was the next step. He'd seen the signs in the South Pacific seas; humanity still strived in desperation, but in despair, they gave up entirely and no longer fought for the need to survive. Those in despair were already dead men, like Mike packed in the snow on the mountain.

Bishop stayed to the shoulder of Coeur d'Alene Lake Drive, or rather the area right above where the road should have been because the road itself wasn't visible. As he continued into more populated areas, the houses that lined the streets looked deserted. If there were people inside of them, they were hiding out. To the north, several more shots rang out only a few streets away, and before he realized it, he had his AR out by his side. "Come on, Jake. Just a little farther," he urged. "Let's get you to Tubbs Hill."

Tubbs Hill was the area's requisite hiking trail region. The tall pines there were left intact, growing on a large round rocky peninsula covered in trees that seemed to float out from the mainland. Once in the wooded area, Bishop continued to the other side where he could stand and watch the south side of the resort area and still be hidden from view. The wind picked up off the south end of the frozen lake, and Bishop shuddered. Inside of his coat's inner pocket, he broke open a large warming pack and shook the ingredients around, then replaced the thin bag inside of the nylon of his inner pockets. He wouldn't freeze, at least. When he lifted the binoculars to his eyes, he found expensive boats haphazardly frozen in the ice. It seemed no one had had enough notice of the storm to stow them away properly. Then he saw something dark lying on the pier. And then there was another one. There were bodies out there lying in the open. Their clothes on their backs rippled in the wind, which was now coming in sharp gusts.

A sudden flash of a weapon's fire came from around the east side of the tower. A man in uniform shot at someone on the west side of the building, and then behind him a group of men all dressed in the same black uniform began shooting at the uniformed officer.

Bishop watched as he lost his cover and ran out onto the ice and made it as far as the boardwalk of the main pier, but then he was out in the open with no cover at all. Bishop's gloved hand squeezed his rifle, but not knowing who the bad guys were, he held back. More shots rang out as three men pursued the man running out on the ice. *Rat-tat-tat*…the man dropped down after shots stitched through his back. His weapon skidded out several feet in front of him.

"We got him!" one of the men yelled to someone near the shore. "Tell Ramsey he's the last of them. The town's ours now."

Bishop moved his binoculars to the south as the three men patted down the body of their enemy, took his firearm, and walked back. Their voices traveled easily over the frozen ice. They took short steps in an effort to not slip. One guy gave orders to the others, saying,

"We've got this now." Another man asked, "What about Spokane? When they hear, they'll send someone."

"Spokane has their own problems. Ramsey knows what he's doing." He put his arm behind the other guy's head. "Dave, don't question him. Not if you want to keep your family alive. Understand?"

The younger man hesitated for a moment but then nodded. They followed the third guy, walking back to the resort as another gust of sharp, cold wind blew by them. Bishop tightened his coat around himself.

There was something screwed up in the way they were behaving. They wore black uniforms, but they were different from the police officer that they killed. Bishop returned his view to the body on the ice again and magnified the binoculars to get a closer look at the dead man. His uniform was also black, but stitched across the shoulder in gold thread was spelled *Coeur d'Alene Police Department.* "Damn."

He focused on the retreating men again, who were just entering the building. Were those guys just hotel security? Bishop wasn't sure, and he'd never known them to carry arms before. The door closed hard. It was impossible to see inside of the hotel's glass, but he knew they'd have an unobstructed view of him if he broke his cover.

Now the streets were quiet. Bishop felt like he'd come at the end of a battle, and from the looks of the bodies lying in the open, he was probably right. Bishop wasn't prepared for this. He knew now who controlled the city—their leader was a guy named Ramsey. Though he had the information he came for, he had to return to Maeve for now. Bishop needed to head back to camp before the short day turned to night so that he could keep her safe…and so that he could plan how to take back the town.

Chapter 22

Louna coughed from the cave room, and when she did, the jagged sound of it made Maeve cringe while she kept watch at the doorway. Then Louna coughed again and couldn't seem to catch her breath.

Maeve had no choice but to leave her post to aid the child. Panicking because she couldn't breathe, Louna began hyperventilating and coughing in intervals. Maeve rushed to her and pulled her up from the pillow where she was lying. "Louna, it's all right," she soothed as she patted her back. Ben sat up, whipping his eyes toward Louna and looking worried. "Get a cup of water, Ben," Maeve said, and he scampered out of the room.

Louna was now crying through the coughing fit, and Maeve picked her up quickly and swung her around to cradle her in her lap. "Louna," she said sternly, "calm down. You'll make it worse. Breathe…breathe…that's it. Just calm down," she encouraged in a soothing tone. She had to get the girl's attention. She was leading into hysterics, and nothing good came from hysterics, or at least that's what Maeve's mother used to say. "That's it. You're doing better," Maeve said when the girl's breathing slowed. Ben stood at her side with a cup filled with water. He stood tentative, casting worried glances at the girl in his mother's arms.

"She's fine, Ben," she said as she took the cup and held it to the girl's lips. Louna had to slow her breathing even more as she took sips of the water.

"See, she's better now."

"I want…my…mom," Louna cried, and large pools of tears filled her eyes.

Maeve held her close. Louna's voice still sounded rough and raw, and she was warm from a low temperature. "I know, sweetheart, but you're fine now. Why don't you try to sleep a little longer?"

The girl cried for a bit more, and when she settled down, Maeve moved her to the cot again, and she buried her face into the tearstained pillow.

Maeve patted her back as she fell back to sleep.

"Mom, why can't we bring her back to her family?" Ben whispered.

Maeve motioned for her son to come closer to the front room. "I don't think her family made it out of the fire, Ben."

He looked back at the girl lying on the cot in the back room. "So she's an orphan?"

Maeve shook her head. "I don't know. We'll find out in a few days. Bishop went to town to check out things down there. We'll return there when it's safe. Hopefully we can find her relatives when we do."

Ben nodded as if he understood. She wasn't certain he did, but then again, her son had already lost one parent; maybe he understood more than she gave him credit for. Adults didn't have a monopoly on pain, which was something she needed to keep in mind.

A gust of wind rattled the door then. She and Ben both shuddered, and then she realized she needed to get back to her post.

"When's this going to stop, Mom?"

Maeve moved back to the doorway and held the rifle in her hand. "I don't know, son. Bishop believes this will last for years to come. He said we're in a mini ice age now. It's the same thing that the weatherman referred to as the Maunder Minimum."

"Why can't we go into town?"

"Because those men that burned down Louna's house also burned down ours. You remember that?"

He nodded. Maeve hated that the memory would be etched in his mind—armed men blowing out their front window as they fled into the night. If it wasn't for Bishop, she and her son would likely be dead by now, she realized.

The door racketed in the wind. When she looked outside, the snow blew so hard she couldn't even see the trees across the small clearing. Not long before, she'd seen them waving in the wind. To think that Bishop was out in that mess…She worried about this stranger because he'd kept her and the children alive over the past few days. She needed him…and that thought alone scared her more than anything else. She was a grieving widow. That had been her identity over the past year, and now here she was worrying about another man, a friend of her dead husband's.

Ben wandered into the cave room again to check on Louna. He'd become protective of the girl since the moment he had to check her pulse. She thought it was sweet in a way but awful in another. What if this world was one where you lost your loved ones more so than their old reality? She couldn't bear her son going through the grief she held for his father.

Ben pulled the covers up over the girl's shoulders and tucked them in around her. When the wind blew again and the door rattled, Maeve watched her son. Then suddenly, she felt the door rattle deliberately harder, and a strange man's breath leached through the cracks and onto her neck.

"Let me in!"

Chapter 23

On a crisp fall morning, the sun shone bright, and David was enjoying his morning as he read the local newspaper, which was a luxury. Newspapers were a thing of the past and to purchase a printed subscription cost quite a high fee now, but he loved the feel of the paper between his fingers and sorting through the pages rather than swiping on a screen.

Of course, he also owned the local newspaper, and because it was one of his family's many businesses he still demanded the printed format despite the lack of cost effectiveness. He reached for his orange juice and took a sip. The sun warmed the back of his neck. He looked out over the marina, watching a few of the boats heading out for a day on the lake. It would be one of the last nice days of the season.

At sixty-three, David Geller II had stopped trying to live up to his father's name. The mogul who built the empire by Lake Coeur d'Alene proved to be a man impossible to emulate, and yet the best David could do was uphold all his father had achieved. That was the way of things in his mind. He would never be as great a man as his father was, but then again, he loved the man and was proud to call him Dad.

He'd died peacefully in his sleep a decade before, but David still thought of the man every single day, and why not? Everything about his life now revolved around what had taken a lifetime to accomplish. He was merely the caretaker now. The caretaker of the Geller dynasty.

David brushed away an errant fly as he sat on the balcony of his penthouse at the top of the resort tower. He was only going to be there for a few days on business. He and his family called Arizona home now. David was never in favor of having his children grow up in Coeur d'Alene among the shadows that he contended with even now. He wanted his children to grow up somewhere where their mistakes weren't reported in the daily small-town paper. Where if they went over the speed limit occasionally it wasn't reported by everyone who was watching them. No, he had men to oversee everything now. They were capable and so was he…from afar. The gem by the lake was in good hands, and though he was still CEO of the private company that owned the family's entities, Roman was the true man behind the machine.

"Sir." Austin Sanchez, David Geller's personal assistant, stepped out of the door from the penthouse and onto the balcony. "You have a nine-fifteen with Mr. Roman, sir."

David checked his platinum watch on his wrist, not quite believing he'd been sitting out there enjoying his morning for quite that long. "Sure, send him in."

Austin disappeared inside the penthouse, and a few seconds later Roman stepped outside onto the patio and walked toward David. Though Roman ran things with precision, David found him to be a difficult man. He often disagreed with him over minor changes and had to reprimand Roman by reminding him who was actually in charge. He overlooked the challenges because Roman did the job well, even in spite of him questioning his authority too often.

That's why David was here, to check on Roman. Overseeing that his decisions were, in fact, being put into action.

"Good morning, Mr. Geller," Ramsey Roman said.

David flipped his sunglasses up onto the top of his head. He wanted to see the man before him clearly. Roman was dressed in a shirt and tie. His black hair always combed back straight, his face clean shaven, and his dark eyes drilled into whomever he looked at. David often found the younger man intimidated most people. He looked like a mob boss, and perhaps that's why things were done so efficiently. No one questioned him. His voice was booming and relentless, and he had no qualms about using it to thrash insubordinates.

David hated yelling. He wasn't suited to arguments. He paid people to do that kind of thing.

"Good morning, Roman. How are things?"

Roman took the opposite seat at the table and pulled out the tablet he carried around with him always. He flipped through a few apps.

David folded up the newspaper and set it down on the table. Watching Roman with feigned interest, he then wiped his mouth on a napkin. Another boat caught his attention as it left the marina and sailed out to the south side of the lake. David longingly thought what a great afternoon it would be to feel the cool spray against his skin while the sun beat down and the refreshing breeze came in off the lake.

"There're a few things we should discuss, sir," Roman said to recapture David's attention.

"Well, go ahead. I'm listening."

Roman nodded. "The hotel is at eighty-three percent capacity this morning. Not unusual for this time of year as the weather changes. The golf course is being readied for the end of the season. The newspaper is reporting steady revenue. In all, nothing out of the ordinary except…"

"Except?" David asked.

"Except that there are weather reports coming in saying that there's a big snowstorm on the way. Very unusual for this time of year."

"Snowstorm? At the end of October?"

"Yes, sir. The meteorologists are scrambling. It might impact the resort's weekend."

"I've grown up here, and I only remember it snowing a few times in October, but not an *actual* snowstorm. Besides, it'll blow over in a few days. Nothing we can't handle. If we lose a few bookings that's nothing to worry about."

Roman looked at him with those dark eyes. He wanted to say something more but held back.

"Winterize the hotel early if you must."

Roman clipped a quick, resolute nod at his boss.

"Is that all?"

"Yes, sir," Roman said and stood.

"Let me know if anything changes."

Roman nodded again and took his leave.

David gazed out at the water as the midmorning sun reflected on the placid waves. Even if there was a snowstorm coming in, the boaters still would have this last glorious day of the season. Though, currently, there wasn't a cloud in sight.

Chapter 24

"Go away!" Maeve screamed through the door. There were three men on the other side, and they continued to push against the gate. The sky had darkened after a brief period of gray, and for over an hour now they'd begged her to let them enter.

"We need to come inside. It's cold. Help us," one of the men pleaded.

"No, I've told you there's nothing for you here. It's just me, and I'm not letting you in. Please go away. I'm sure you can find shelter somewhere else."

It didn't make sense to her. If they really needed somewhere to stay, why didn't they hole up in the stable next door? Not that she wanted them to, but that's what she would have done if she were in the same circumstances.

No, these people were up to no good. She could feel it. The leader's voice made her skin crawl, and the others pleaded with her as if they were taunting her.

Louna was crying now in the back of the cave, and Ben was with her trying to calm her down. She motioned for them to keep quiet, but it was no use.

Through the slats, she saw one of the men eyeballing the inside. She picked up her mug and threw her water at him.

He growled, shaking the water off his face. "She's got babies in there."

Maeve'd had enough. "I said, leave! Leave now, or I'll shoot."

"Darlin', we've got all the time in the world. We're staying right here until you let us inside."

Noticing that the leader was back and the other two were probably hiding out in the stable next door, she realized they were tag-teaming her, and then she heard one of them banging on the wall behind the woodstove. They were inside the stable now, doing their best to scare her. She had no idea where Bishop was or when he'd be back, and she was afraid that they'd shoot him if he showed up and didn't know they were there.

"I have nothing for you here," she tried again. "I have no food for you to take. Go away."

"Oh, you have something for us, darlin'."

She shuddered. These guys were the scum who hung out in the lowest parts of town. The ones who were picked up constantly for heroin and other such nefarious activities. Every town had them, even Coeur d'Alene, and in a time of crisis they always came out of the woodwork to take advantage of those who worked for a living.

She was in real danger. They continued to bang on the walls. There was no other exit to escape from, but they could break down the wood partition between the two structures where the woodstove stood. She'd have to shoot them before they could get to her, or they might hurt the children.

"Look, I'm armed. If you keep this up, I'm going to have to shoot. Do you understand?"

They didn't answer, but they continued to tear at the wall. Dust fell from the ceiling. This was deliberate, and she couldn't believe they would take advantage of a woman in a desperate situation. "Stop! I mean it. Stop the banging!"

They still didn't heed her warnings. Then, the wood wall rattled near the woodstove. Vibrating with each slam of a fist, the planks jostled to the other side.

Terrified, she left the doorway to shore up the wall. "I've had it!" she snapped when a slate gave way just above her head. A large dirty hand shot through the opening suddenly and grabbed a handful of her hair. She pulled to the other side, but it was too late.

Chapter 25

Roman sat at his desk in an office that most men would kill for just for the view alone, but Roman didn't care about the view beyond its necessity. He couldn't own the view of the lake so blue, like a sapphire serpent that sprawled into the evergreen forest. He paged through his tablet watching weather alerts. The boss wasn't worried, but he was. This storm looked big, really big, and he'd never seen anything like it in the twenty-three years he'd worked for Mr. Geller. He'd given his life to the Gellers except for the stint he did in the war to serve his country. The senior Geller promised him compensation when he returned, and he kept his word to a point.

Roman despised David. He was a milquetoast master and wasn't at all what his father once was. Roman knew the late Mr. Geller would have taken the big storm seriously. He knew him well enough to realize this was an exceptional emergency and that the old man would have insisted he ran the disaster preparedness for the whole town himself. Geller should be making disaster preparedness decisions, but he'd left it up to Roman to deal with as if it were any other seasonal storm.

Roman made a few calls. He ordered storm shutters for the windows and told the dockmaster to call all the boat owners and urge them to get their crafts put away immediately. "We're not responsible for the damage to their boats if they're destroyed in the storm," he said to the manager. "I don't care. Our insurance doesn't cover it." Another call came, and he knew it was probably the newspaper. He nodded to the guy on the phone. "That's right. One call to each owner, then move on. It's supposed to snow tonight…I don't care, Jim. It's their responsibility. All right," he said and ended the call.

No doubt he'd hear about it when one of the multimillion-dollar boats in the marina sustained damage. He'd point them to their phone records. All that was needed was an attempt to contact, and even then they weren't responsible, but it was a base he needed to cover.

By the end of the day, Roman had the storm shutters recovered from storage and ordered them to be installed overnight if need be. The guests would complain, but he had to protect Geller's assets. The next major issue was Geller himself. He shouldn't be here. Roman had work to do, and Geller was in the way. The last thing he needed was Geller here telling him what to do in a crisis. No, the man had to go, one way or another.

"Sir, the sheriff returned your call. He says they're busy, but he'll call back sometime tomorrow," said his assistant.

"Busy?"

"Yes, sir. He's on vacation in Rockford on his ranch. He said he'd come back into town next week."

Roman nodded. "Then get his deputy on the phone. They need to get busy making preparations. I'm sure they don't even have the sand trucks working or anything. Do I have to do everything in this damn town? Did you get the cruise boats into dry dock?"

"They're working on it now, sir."

Roman's cell phone rang then. It was Geller's assistant, Austin. "Ah, damn. I don't have time for him," he said but flipped the phone on anyway. "Yes?"

"It's Mr. Geller, sir. He noticed the cruise boats going into dry dock, and he wants to know why?"

Roman blew out a frustrated breath. "Tell him the storm is coming and it's worse than we thought. Tell him I've called for his helicopter to take him to the airport. His plane is waiting. He needs to get back to Arizona where it's safer before the storm hits. This is an emergency. Tell him because I don't have time to talk to him right now."

He ended the call and ran out of the office. There was yelling coming from the lobby of the hotel, and he'd had about enough of people not doing what he'd ordered them to do the first time.

Chapter 26

They had a hold of his mother's hair.

Too late she'd realized that when the man grabbed her from the other side of the wall, she'd dropped the rifle she was holding. The rifle landed on the floor in front of her. She screamed when they yanked her against the wood so hard her head slammed into the wall, and dirty hands clawed from the hole the bad men had made in order to break another section free so that they could gain further entry.

"Mom!" Ben yelled and ran partway into the room. His eyes were on the rifle.

"No, stay back!" she yelled, crying out while she reached her arms toward the rifle. Ben tried to run inside to retrieve the rifle but each time he attempted to do so, she waved her right hand at him and screamed, "Please stay back!"

Another piece of the wood broke free, and his mother screamed out as another hand reached around and grabbed her around the neck. She fought them, trying to pull away, but they scratched and tore at her skin. There were three arms through the hole in the wall, and Ben didn't know what to do.

He had to do something. He looked back at Louna screaming on the bed behind him and something in him snapped. He ran for the rifle as his mother's eyes widened and she screamed in horror. Time seemed to have slowed down. He scrambled for the rifle and shook as he lifted the heavy weight of the Ruger Mini 14 rifle with his small arms and pointed the barrel end beside his mother's head.

In the hole, a man's face appeared, sneering at him and laughing. He levered the rifle against his slight shoulder. His mother kicked and screamed but couldn't pull free. She was choking with the effort to free herself.

Ben aimed at the man like he'd seen Bishop do trying to balance the weight of the barrel. His mother's red hair flew all over struggling—he pulled the trigger.

A blast shuddered behind the wall. Suddenly all the screaming ceased with the loud explosion. Then his ears began to ring loudly. One of the arms dropped down.

Another blast sounded, though Ben wasn't aiming at all this time. Then another and the sneering man disappeared from view. His mother then fell to the ground. Ben dropped the rifle and skittered over to her side. She clutched her son in her arms. Blood trailed from scratches in her neck, and suddenly he realized he must have shot her. "Did I shoot *you*?" Horror spread over his face. He was confused. He heard the shots but never felt the blast.

"Hey, you guys all right?"

Ben stood up. "Bishop!"

He'd unlocked the door and quickly come through. "I saw their trail. I came as soon as I could."

Ben watched as Bishop looked from his mother on the floor to the hole in the wall and dropped to his knees. Bishop picked up his mother easily from the floor and brought her into the cave. "Ben, get some water and a towel."

He put her down gently on a cot and then picked up Louna, who was hysterical, and brought her over to his mother's side. She automatically began soothing the girl.

Ben brought the water and towel to Bishop. The big man soaked the rag and wiped his mother's neck and chest where they'd left gouges in her skin. "You're going to be all right, Maeve," Bishop said.

"I couldn't do it," she said, looking at him and then at Louna. "They would have killed us all."

"Yes, they would have, but they didn't."

Ben felt guilty he hadn't been the one to stop the men from hurting his mother after all. The rifle didn't work. He didn't know how to use it, and that was something he never wanted to happen again.

He couldn't use the words. His throat felt thick and dry suddenly. He patted Bishop on the thigh.

"What is it, buddy?"

"I…I want to use the gun. Show me."

Bishop regarded him for a second.

Ben looked to his mother and then back at Bishop. He needed to help protect them. They'd almost killed her. He'd have to know these things to survive.

"I'll teach you. Don't worry."

Chapter 27

"Come home, please!"

"I...I am. I feel like I need to stay here and supervise, though."

"I'm sure Roman has it under control, dear. There's nothing you can do there that you can't do from here. He's only a phone call away."

Geller's wife was frantic after she'd heard the news broadcast. Everywhere there was a news blitz about the coming winter storm and unusual weather activity. He watched the television as a scientist tried to explain the Maunder Minimum.

"But if this was such a big deal, why are we just learning about this phenomenon?" the news anchor asked.

The scientist pushed his glasses up the bridge of his nose. *"That's a good question. The science has been around for decades. This phenomenon just wasn't a popular notion."*

"What do you mean? Are you saying most scientists didn't believe in the Maunder Minimum?"

"What I'm saying is that since climate change is accepted science the theory of Maunder Minimum just didn't sell. I mean, we went from global warming to climate change, and the Maunder Minimum was at the other end of the explanation. That the world was not getting warmer but in fact getting colder due to the lack of sun activity was less popular than the notion that man was destroying the earth's atmosphere."

"So, though we know this has happened in the past, the theory was disputed in favor of climate change."

"Well," the scientist said, *"climate change is something that encompasses the Maunder Minimum. The earth heats some years and cools inexplicably during others. We've had years without a summer in history as well. The notion that overall the earth is heating instead of cooling is just more popular without muddling society's take on climate change. We just don't try to confuse them with things like the Maunder Minimum."*

"This is crazy," Geller said and switched off the TV. His wife was still talking on the phone, though he had no idea what she was going on about. "I'm coming home, dear. Apparently, I have no choice. The decision was made for me. Roman ordered the helicopter, and the plane is waiting. I'll be there in a few hours."

"They said it will snow here too. Here, in November, in *Arizona*?" his wife said.

"Well, it won't stick for long. We might as well enjoy it. I'll see you soon," Geller said as Roman came through his bedroom door.

"Ready, sir?" Roman asked as Austin picked up Geller's packed luggage and headed out the door ahead of them.

"Yes, though I wish you'd consulted with me first, Roman."

"I thought it was important, sir, to make sure you were safe. They may not allow planes to fly in a few hours—that's what they're saying at the airport."

"I'm leaving Austin here. He has family nearby. I want you to look out for him. He'll use my office to work on my memoirs while I'm gone."

Roman nodded that he understood.

They walked the short flight of stairs to the roof where the noise became deafening. The helicopter's engine roared in the high winds; it was suddenly very cold when Roman opened the door. Though the day was beautiful before with the sun shining on the lake, Geller was shocked now to see formidable gray skies looming in the distance.

He looked toward the lake with his hand shading his eyes. The waves were choppy. Geller's forehead creased. He had never seen such a swing in conditions in one morning. Where he'd sat earlier in the morning, the chairs were turned over and lying on their sides. The table lay at an angle.

"This way, Mr. Geller." Roman urged him toward the helipad.

He walked against the force of the wind, his shirt rippling against his skin. Geller stopped before getting into the helicopter. He'd suddenly realized how drastic things were. He looked at Roman's determined face and grabbed his hand. "You've got everything under control?"

"I do, sir. You go on. I can handle this."

Their hands parted, and Geller nodded and then scrambled inside the copter. He knew he was more of a hindrance than a help and trusted that Roman had everything under control. He should get out of the way so the man could do his job.

Roman cleared the helipad and watched briefly as the helicopter lifted and flew west toward the airport. Hopefully Geller would reach his destination, but then again, Roman didn't give a damn if he did or didn't.

Chapter 28

"What's it like down there?" Maeve asked the man who had saved her life yet again as he applied antibacterial ointment to the many scratches around her neck.

"It's a mess. The lake is completely frozen over, which is good and bad. We can cross the ice more easily, but I'm pretty sure the nonnative fish are most likely dead since it froze over so fast, and that limits our water sources."

"Well, we have all this snow we can melt for water," she said as Bishop slid ointment with his finger over a long scratch. She sucked in a quick breath.

"I'm sorry. I don't have anything to apply it with, but my hands are clean."

"That's OK."

He continued applying the ointment and talked as he did to distract her from the pain. "It's true that we have water, but the town's in danger. I don't know who's taken over, but the police are not running things. There's a lot of shooting and bodies in the streets. I have to go back there, Maeve."

She grabbed his wrist when he said those words she dreaded.

"Please. Please don't leave us here alone." She shook her head. "Please don't," she begged him. She shuddered at the memory of the men who'd attacked her.

He looked at her elegant hand wrapped around his wrist and placed his hand over hers. "Maeve, I have to go back. In order to keep you and the children alive, I have to get down there and stop whoever has taken over. People are dying down there. We can't stay here forever. This is only the beginning. The weather is going to get much, much worse than it is now."

Her eyes widened with fear. "How much worse can it get?"

He pulled away from her and stood. "The temperature will drop further, and it will stay that way for a long time. I doubt we'll see another summer for a few years, in fact. There will be no crops next year to harvest, nothing to sustain people. They'll starve to death after they run out of supplies. There's not enough insulation here. I need to get you and the kids into a safer fortified building." He turned away from her with his hands on his hips. "It might take me a few days, Maeve."

"Can't we come with you? What if…what if you get killed?"

"I won't. I can't," Bishop said and grabbed his coat and went outside. He'd already disposed of the bodies of the three men who had tried to break in. He'd also repaired the hole in the wall from the stable side.

The snow had briefly subsided, so he took advantage of the visibility and went to the cliff's ledge with his night vision binoculars to get a brief glimpse of the troubled town below. He couldn't tell much from here, but the fires would tell him that either things were continuing to deteriorate or they'd stabilized.

By the time he made it to the cliff, he'd found that there wasn't a big difference from the last time he'd checked. Where one house fire was out, another had begun. He could only imagine the pain and turmoil the people were in. Not only did they have to contend with this natural disaster, but some criminal faction had taken advantage of it as well.

"Not for long," Bishop swore. "I'm coming. Your days are numbered."

A twig snapped behind him, and Bishop turned on his heel, weapon drawn and crouched all in one fluid motion. A man dressed in furs stood just inside the tree line, also armed and aiming. It took Bishop less than a second to see the man dressed in furs from head to foot was none other than Jax.

"You'd be a dead man."

Bishop stood. "So would you, Jax. Maybe a hair later." His heart pounded a little less, but the sudden adrenaline rushing in his veins without an outlet made his hands shake.

"Came to tell you…too many people in these woods."

Bishop walked half the distance through the snow to meet him. "Yeah, I've seen them too. Found a dead man just a mile west yesterday."

"Like a spigot been turned on. Needs to stop," Jax said and spit a large wad of saliva into the snow beside where he stood.

Jax was agitated, and Bishop worried how the old man would handle the change in the woods. He wasn't like most men. Handling society at large wasn't in Jax. He needed solitude to survive.

Nodding his head in the direction of the troubled town in the valley below, Bishop explained the situation to him. Giving him a reason why the people were now invading his forest.

Watching Jax's hardened eyes change, Bishop wasn't sure if the old man had sympathy for humanity at all, but his expression told him that if he did he kept the sentiment veiled.

"You going down there?"

Bishop nodded.

"Stop them."

"I'll try."

Jax's menacing eyes shot daggers at him now.

"Don't come back till you do." He turned then, and Bishop watched the cranky old buzzard disappear into the forest as silently as he'd come.

He thought it odd that Jax never inquired about the girl's health or, for that matter, his own. He could never figure him out, but that's why he lived out in the forest to begin with—no one could figure out Jax. He was an anomaly in society, and if he had to live among men, he would do so only in a padded room—that much Bishop was sure of. And what a tragedy that would be.

The real question was, could he leave Maeve and the children again and expect them to be safe with so many people fleeing the town? Images of Maeve's red hair in the hands of the attackers flashed before him. His stomach clenched when he couldn't help but think of what they would have done to her had he been delayed for a minute longer. Oddly, it was their smell that had first alerted him. He'd seen many tracks through the snow, but there was something about a man who hadn't bathed in days, that rotted reek, that alarmed him as he approached his own camp knowing they were there.

"Bishop."

He'd heard the door open when he neared the camp and wasn't surprised to see her outline in the doorway. "I heard you talking to someone and saw Jax. I...didn't want to come out then. Can I please talk to you about going into town?"

Visibly shaking, Maeve's red hair, so vibrant, stood out like a wild rose in a desert. The marks on the tender skin of her slender neck made him ache in a way that made him want to murder the three assailants all over again. *How dare they lay a hand on her?*

With a rough voice, he said, "He's gone now."

She stood near him. The wind gusted into her face, almost taking her breath away. Taking a step to shield her, he said, "You should go back inside."

"I have to ask you, Bishop, please. Don't leave us here alone again. Please bring us down with you. I promise we'll stay out of the way. Can't you leave us somewhere nearby? There are too many desperate people now."

Lines etched her forehead. Trembling, she begged him. She looked utterly terrified. And she was right. There were too many people haunting the woods, too many looking for shelter away from the dangers of the town below. They were capable of anything. She'd nearly died.

He looked past her to Ben's image in the doorway. "I have a place. I have to go there anyway. It's just a storage unit. Heated, but not heated enough. It'll be hard to keep warm, and it's not safe either. But...I can put you and the kids there while I do what I need to do."

She nodded and even smiled. Relief relaxed the tension on her face. "Thank you," she said, and he ushered her inside the cabin, built in front of a cave, once again as another gust of cold, hard wind howled through.

Chapter 29

Roman quickly called a meeting of the hotel managers in the largest conference room before Geller had even left. There was little time to prepare. The storm was coming fast. They were waiting for him, seated in soft leather chairs around an enormous oblong table. When Roman walked in, they turned in his direction.

"Get these people out of here!" he yelled to the hotel manager. "All of them if you can."

"What should I say, sir?"

Roman took a frustrated breath. "Tell them Armageddon is coming. Hell, I don't care. Tell them there's a weather emergency and they have a window to get home now or they're stuck here. That's the truth." He leveled a steely gaze at the manager. "Now go!"

Everyone watched as the suit scrambled out the door.

Roman turned his attention to the newspaper. "Andrew, put out all the emergency services' contact information. Link any information you can find about emergency preparedness. No one goes to work, to school—"

"Sir, it's up to the superintendent to call off school."

"Has he?"

"Uh, no. There was a two-hour late start today."

"Tell that jackass school is out for the foreseeable future. What does he think he's doing? Kids will freeze to death walking home." Roman shook his head in disgust. "Schools are shut down *now*! Make sure you stress the seriousness of the weather situation. This is going to be extremely dire. The city needs to shut completely down."

"Yes, sir," said the editor and left.

There was always a man at the table the others didn't know. He never answered when asked what his position was, but he was dressed like them and sat with them anytime a meeting was called. He'd become Roman's right-hand man, and he was always the last to leave the room.

"I want this city totally halted."

147

One manager leaned up in his chair. "What about the mayor, sir? Isn't he supposed to deal with this kind of thing?"

"Do you see him preparing for anything?"

"Well, no, I...but he's the mayor. He said it's going to be a little freak storm. Nothing to worry about—it'll blow over in a day or two."

Roman rubbed his chin and said with increasing intensity so that he was nearly spitting on the man who'd asked, "I don't give a damn what he said. We protect Geller's interest. That means we shore up this building, the marina, the golf course, the newspaper, and all the other little businesses under Geller's name. Understand?"

"Yes, sir!" he said and left the room quickly with the others.

The remaining man at the table with Roman leaned back in his leather chair after reaching inside of his jacket and pulling out a cigarette and lighter. He lit up while Roman thumbed through his tablet, began typing for a moment, and then regarded the man.

"How are sales, Frank?"

"Not bad," he said. Smoke drifted up and around his head. "You really care about the kids?" He chuckled, surprised that Roman took an interest.

"The more people stay home, the more who are off my streets and out of my way."

Roman leaned back in his chair, matching the relaxed attitude of the other man. "How will the weather affect business?"

Frank smirked. "Depends on how bad things get. We may have to diversify if conditions deteriorate the way you say they will."

Roman nodded. "They will, Frank. So diversify is what you'll do. If the cell towers go down, I want you here. We have backup radios, but I may need your expertise. Don't stray far."

"Yes, boss."

Roman returned to his tablet, and Frank stood and walked by. He clapped Roman on the shoulder as he left the room.

Frank was one man he could depend on. He wasn't afraid to get his hands dirty, and he handled the underground. That was a side business Geller wasn't privy to. The underground was Roman's empire, and he ran that empire like a fine oiled machine with the unwitting assistance of Geller himself.

Chapter 30

"This is the safety switch." Bishop pointed to the lever on the Ruger Mini 14 rifle. "This is why you couldn't shoot the rifle. When that switch is in place, it doesn't shoot. That's why it's called *safety*. Anytime a rifle isn't in use, it must be in safety. Got it?"

Ben nodded. Bishop led the young boy through the procedures. The wind picked up again, and snow flurries were coming in sideways—making visibility an issue—but the training had to continue no matter the conditions.

"You never point a gun at anyone you don't intend to kill. Plain and simple. Don't play around with guns. You don't warn someone with a gun, you shoot them with it and you shoot to kill. Understand?"

Ben nodded again. His mother remained in the cabin with Louna. When Bishop left with Ben to teach him a few things she was reluctant, but he made her see things his way with one phrase. "He learns or he dies."

She'd nodded then, even with tears in her eyes. The world was different, and Bishop knew that if Roger were alive he too would have made sure the young boy knew how to defend himself and his family. It's what men did in real life. They taught their sons how to survive and to protect those they loved. There were no politics involved; all political correctness was lost when survival was at play. This was the real world. To survive you had to defend yourself and your family or you ceased to exist. It was a cut-and-dried methodology.

"Now, when you shoot, the stock is going to buck at your shoulder. It might hurt. It might leave a bruise later, but you have to ride it out." He levered the rifle's barrel on a cold stone boulder and showed the boy how to hold the rifle against his small frame. "You're not fully grown yet, so you'll need to improvise because of your small size. Do what you have to do. Now, never put your finger in the trigger guard unless you're going to fire. No fingers allowed inside that hole, ever, unless you mean business. Now look through the sights. That's it. Now, sight the can on the rock. See it? Are you going to take the shot?"

Ben nodded.

"Really? What's on the other side of the can? People?"

"No, just trees."

"Are you sure?"

"No."

"What if your mom was taking a walk back there? Would you shoot the bad guy in front of her with your mom behind him?"

"No."

"That's right. Even if you're aiming at someone with others around, you don't take the shot if you might hit someone else. Never take a shot like that. That's not a clean shot. Understand?"

"Yes."

"Good. OK, the shot is *clear*. There's no one back there. Your enemy is that can. He's the bad guy. What do you need to do to take the shot?"

"Take it off safety?" Ben asked.

"That's right. Go ahead."

Ben's little fingers worked the safety switch right on the outside of the trigger guard. His finger pushed it away with an audible click. Bishop took a deep breath. The by was so young. He seemed very mature for his age, but his size…he was tiny and not nearly strong enough to handle the gun in an emergency situation.

"Good. It'll get easier with practice, but don't practice with the rifle inside or when there's anyone on the other side of that barrel, clear?"

Ben nodded again.

"All right. Take aim. Safety off. Target in sight. Now take in a breath, let it out, and then hold it as you let your finger in the trigger guard and pull."

Ben did exactly as he was told, and when the rifle went off the hilt rammed into his right shoulder, pushing the boy backward and nearly toppling him over from his seated position.

He jerked and looked up at Bishop in shock.

"Good job, kid," Bishop said and saw that the can had flown off from the impact. "You hit it."

Ben rubbed his shoulder a bit but pulled up the corner of his mouth into a smile.

"Really, that was great. I wish we could get more practice in, but we don't want to draw more attention to our area. What's the first thing you do when you're done shooting?"

"Put the safety back on."

"Exactly. Good boy. You learn fast," he said and tousled the kid's hair. It was way too cold to stay outside any longer than necessary, and though it was a short lesson, Bishop brought Ben back inside to his mother.

She stood inside holding Louna. Both of them looked startled from the rifle shot's blast.

"It's OK. He did great."

"I shot the gun, Mom!"

"And more importantly, he hit the can too," Bishop said as if they were father and son coming home from target practice. What a shame he was teaching the boy to survive during a time of crisis instead of as a life skill that every boy needs to know in ordinary times.

"That's…good, Ben," Maeve said reluctantly. She stared straight at Bishop.

"We've got to pack now. This rifle is yours, Ben. It's the lightest one I've got, and there's plenty of ammo. You also have your Ruger," he reminded Maeve.

She nodded and finished adjusting a spare coat of Bishop's for Louna to wear for their trip down the mountain. The jacket fell past Louna's knees, and since the child also wore several layers of Bishop's thermal shirts she looked like a large roly-poly. Still weak with a cough and a slight fever, Louna wasn't as ready for the hour-long trip by horseback through a blizzard as Maeve would have liked, but safety first. And Maeve couldn't imagine staying in the cabin after what had happened last time. Usually independent, she'd never in her life felt as scared and as helpless to defend her child as she had then.

She put Louna down and picked up the bags that Bishop packed. He brought Jake around and attached a sled on the back for the horse to pull. Maeve handed him the things they were taking, and then he put Ben and Louna near the top of the sled, laying layers of blankets over them. He took Maeve around to the side next, motioning for her to get up into the saddle.

"I can walk with you," she said.

Bishop shook his head no. "If I need you to get out of there in a hurry, Jake has more escape power. It's a long walk, and you don't know where to step through the snow. Plus, you'll be our lookout up there. Keep your eyes open and your gun ready."

"I don't think I could shoot anyone," she whispered out of the kids' earshot.

Bishop watched her. Her eyes were wild with fear. She was scared through, and there wasn't much he could do about that. "Maeve, what happened before, those men…you should have shot them as soon as they entered the clearing. Picked them off one by one."

"I can't…I'm not like you. I don't know how to do these things."

He made his voice calm, knowing if he lowered it she would relax a little. "You want those kids to survive? I know you do. I can't be everywhere. You can't let anyone get too close. Shoot before they do." She continued to shake before him like a leaf. He reached for her and held her in his arms. "Anyone would be afraid, Maeve. I still get afraid. It means you're human."

She calmed down with his touch. Her cold hands warmed against his chest. Her stiff back melted against his strong arms. Her breath brushed hot against his neck.

"I'll try."

He'd made a plan and was packed and ready to go…but now, though, he only wanted to hold her close to him. The problem was, she was Maeve, Roger's wife, but no one had made him feel this way before. He stepped away from her gently and looked into her eyes. "Let's go," he said and knelt down for her step one foot into his open palms. When she did, she swung her right leg over the saddle. He wrapped another blanket around her and then led Jake down the path, checking over his precious cargo while also constantly scanning the surroundings.

With her scent still lingering on him, he hoped it would remain as a reminder of what was at stake.

Chapter 31

A few days later, Roman was never surer of the situation than he was now. Most of the hotel residents left, and he was glad. As long as they were out the door, he didn't care if they ended up stranded alongside the ice-covered streets—so long as they weren't staying in his hotel or trying to bum on the streets of Coeur d'Alene.

After three days and nights, the power diminished. The cell phone towers no longer worked, and the police department was utterly useless. That's when Roman decided it was time. Time for him to take over. Enough was enough.

"What about the grocery stores?" Frank asked. "There are no deliveries being made. The highways are shut down. No one is getting through anywhere in the country, let alone here."

"No food deliveries? That sucks," Roman said, "Has the sheriff taken over the grocery stores? I mean, what's in there now is all we have, right? The hotel only stocks a few days at a time."

Frank took a puff off of a cigarette, the smoke swirled upward. "The sheriff is over in Rockford Bay on his ranch. Last time anyone heard from him, there wasn't much he could do. Said the markets were private businesses and he couldn't dictate that they not sell food. Doesn't matter anyway; the grocery stores had runs in the beginning days. What they do have left isn't much. Most of the shelves are bare."

Roman swung his arm toward the urban sprawl to the east of the building out of his conference room window. "So all the grocery stores are out of food?"

Frank nodded. "Looks that way."

Roman paced the floor back and forth. "Highways shut down, no food deliveries, no communication, and no end in sight. They'll all die. Your family…my men. No, this isn't going to happen. Frank, you have boys, right? You've got that team? We've used them before."

"Yeah, sure. There's a network of preppers who are on the radios too. They keep a lot of stuff. They had encouraged everyone else to horde stuff before it was too late."

"Before it was too late?" Roman repeated the statement. "It was too late a few days ago. But that's not how things are going down." Roman continued pacing. "Starting tonight. Hit these hoarders and take everything they have. Any resistance, and they die. Bring everything here. We'll put it in storage. They want to eat, *we* will feed them. I'm not going to have hoarders in my town."

Frank was already up and headed for the door, nearly giddy with anticipation. "Yes, sir."

Chapter 32

Shots rang out that night as three trucks left the scene filled with the bounty of several nearby homes. If the residents didn't comply with Frank's order to hand over their stocked food, he took what meager rations they did have by force. With a bullhorn in one hand, he held onto the back of the truck with the other as he continued to announce, "Turn over your supplies so that we can all survive together. If your neighbor has hidden rations, let us know and we'll be happy to send over a few folks to help them get the items into the community store. No hoarders are allowed. We all must survive."

Having neighbors rat on neighbors was the easiest way to find all the hidden supplies. They carted supplies by the truckload into the hotel basement, where everything was sorted and inventoried. Those who resisted were summarily dragged out of their houses and shot in the streets for everyone to witness. There was no better motivator than fear.

Frank's boys were used to violence. They were those who thrived on the seedier side of life by providing ladies to the more unscrupulous of the resort vacationers. Or for those who wanted more than a little alcohol to soothe their needs. Roman needed Frank because his boss, Geller, refused to see the other side. He was too good for that way of life, and someone had to provide for the wants and needs of rich men beyond Geller's comprehension.

Roman was to Frank as Geller was to Roman; only one was in the observed world, and the other was invisible. Or, more likely, Frank's world was what Geller turned a blind eye to. Whether or not the man was aware of his talents, he didn't know. That was up to Roman. For now, Frank did exactly what Roman wanted, and that was to control the town.

"Frank, the police are right around the corner. They want to know what's going on," one of his workers stated.

"Oh really?" Frank nearly laughed. "I'll tell them what's going on. I'm doing their job—that's what's going on."

Frank walked around the snowmobiles where some of his men were relieving an owner of his supplies while he kept watch and made sure nothing went to hell. Then he went around the corner where a police snowmobile had pulled to the side of the street, hanging back in the shadows. Two officers were waiting for him.

"We have some questions, Frank."

He recognized both of these men. You could say they'd worked together a time or two.

"Hey, fellas. A little brisk, wouldn't you say?"

They both laughed as the snow continued to pile up around them.

"We're getting calls, Frank," said the older officer.

"They keep asking if this is *legal*," a young officer said with a roll of the eyes. "You shot Mr. Henderson—"

"That was self-defense. He pulled the gun on one of my boys. We shot back." Frank said, both of his hands up in a helpless gesture.

The first officer snorted. "Nice one. Look, martial law was issued two days ago, so as far as we're concerned there isn't a problem. But Sheriff Weston from the south side said his people are running out of food already in Rockford Bay, and he wants us to bring some of ours over the lake via snowmobile."

"He wants some of the food?"

"Yeah. He said the residents there are getting really antsy."

"That's too damn bad. I know what Roman will say…hell no."

The second officer agreed. "See, I told you," he said to the first officer.

"We also have a few guys that are saying this is *wrong*."

"What's wrong?"

The first officer twirled his gloved finger in the air. "This, what we're doing."

"What, keeping people alive? Have him come talk to me then. If he has the balls…"

The first officer snorted again. "He might. I don't know."

Frank slapped the younger officer on the shoulder. "Don't sweat it, Luke. Hey, tell my sister I'll be by later with a few things."

"I will, Uncle Frank," he said, and as Frank turned around, the officers mounted their snowmobiles and drove away.

Chapter 33

Bishop left camp this time with a heavy heart, not knowing when he might return. He made sure everything was locked in tight, but that was no guarantee that his supplies would be there when he came back. He couldn't bring all the MREs he wanted and had to make do with the space available.

The other thing was that the little girl was improving every day, which meant she was asking more questions. Questions they couldn't answer for her. He hoped they could find relatives to take her in—as long as she would be safe with them—once they made it safely into town. And now that Ben could shoot, he felt a little relieved while being worried at the same time. Had Bishop come a second later when the three men were attacking Maeve, they would have killed her and the children. He had no doubt about that.

He also had doubts about keeping them in the storage unit. No place was safe enough. They wouldn't survive in these conditions. He had to get into town and take out the man that was killing so many. If he didn't turn things around in Coeur d'Alene, they'd all die, and soon. The temperatures were plummeting even faster than his predictions, and if that were possible, conditions would deteriorate even faster. They needed more resources to survive the cold. Thick insulated walls and running water would be a nice start.

Once they'd left the mountain, he could feel Maeve's increased tension. She sat even more erect, watching everything he could not see. "Just tell me if you see any movement whatsoever," he'd told her. Once they met the frozen ice of the lake, Bishop noted the footprint traffic had increased since the time he'd come before.

Most of the tracks were leaving town, probably in the dead of night and for good reason, but these people were walking into their own deaths and that Bishop was sure of. Anyone exposed out in the open in another week would surely freeze to death, their bodies never to be discovered. No one would ever know what had happened to them—as if they'd vanished. Clouds of steam rose off Jake and Bishop in great puffs the closer they came to town. Bishop, too, was on alert. It was one thing when he was alone—it was another having Maeve and the children with him, which was a vulnerability he had not anticipated. As soon as he neared the maze of storage units, he stopped at the end of one of the long rows and had Maeve step down from the horse. Her legs buckled when she first landed on the ground, so much so that he had to steady her for a long moment until he was sure she wouldn't topple over.

"I'm OK," she whispered.

Then he led Jake inside the storage unit, pulling the sled inside with him. After detaching the sled, they brushed the snow off of the children and lifted the heavy blankets from them. They were toasty with the shared heating units.

Maeve made a pallet near a stack of storage boxes for the kids and covered them up again in hopes of keeping their warmth intact.

"You can still see your breath in here," Bishop said. "I doubt there's power in town anymore." Having first rented the unit when he'd returned from war, it was where he'd kept belongings that he didn't readily need up on the mountain.

Also inside the garage was his snowmobile—of the latest design, before the war made purchasing them forbidden. This one was battery operated, like the old Prius, and it was quiet and stealthy. Only the snow crunching under the cleats announced its presence from afar. The only issue was recharging the battery, but going fifty miles on one charge was sufficient for his needs when he'd purchased it. Luckily, he kept backup batteries for this purpose. Every fall he did the maintenance on the machine in the garage and took it out in the winter on the back hills for days at a time, traveling the deep woods. Though he'd always used it for recreation, this was a job that would require speed and the element of surprise. Lifting the tarp, Bishop's adrenaline began to rush slightly; this machine had a new mission, and he could finally use it for more than traversing the mountains.

He'd kept various items in the storage unit, and the snowmobile was one of them. These were things he didn't need up in the mountains most of the year and only played with them in the few months that winter allowed in most years.

Opening another locker in the storage unit, he took out several rounds of ammunition and two other rifles. One was semiautomatic and as illegal as they came. If Bishop were ever caught, he'd spend a lot of time in prison just for having the thing in his possession…and for a few prize items like smoke grenades and flash bombs. Explosives were something he'd taken the liberty of when he'd had the chance. He and Roger took turns bringing things home secretly, and now was the time to use them. If he'd ever thought of a scenario to use them for, this was it.

Then there were the warming units. Pulling a few more out, he handed them to Maeve. She activated one and stuffed it under the blankets between the kids. He would bring a few with him as well. All of these items had sat dormant for years. Except for engine maintenance, Bishop rarely even came there.

After packing up, he needed only to wait a few minutes for darkness to completely descend. He'd planned to hit up the first person he knew who would know exactly what was going on. Although…he wouldn't be surprised if that man was running the show himself. He'd heard of the guy before, and now that he'd heard his name again from the guys who'd gunned down the police officer, he figured he knew exactly where to find him.

The known drug area of Coeur d'Alene—every town had them—was where the teens went to get high and where they returned until their lives were so screwed up that they kept coming back. Frank ran that part of town. Bishop had never had a reason to engage him before but now was the time.

Once it was pitch dark, Bishop pulled Maeve to the doorway. "Stay absolutely quiet here, no matter what you hear. If someone breaks in, start shooting. You have no other choice. I'll be back as soon as I can."

"Please hurry," she said.

Feeling a strange new sensation, Bishop had the urge to hug her and hold her in his arms. Instead, he squeezed her shoulder. Standing in front of him, she was so frail and terrified, and he'd do anything to change that about her. Without saying another word, he pushed her gently from the doorway, closed and locked the unit, and then covered the tracks they'd made in the snow. Flurries were coming down anyway, but he wanted to ensure he didn't lead anyone to their position.

Maeve and the kids sharing the unit with his horse was less than ideal, but they were at least out of harm's way for the moment. Bishop mounted the snowmobile and drove out the gate, covered his tracks again, and locked the gate behind him. There was no guarantee of safety, but it was the best he could do until he could get the main job done.

Staying to the outer snow-covered streets—only by memory did he even know where they were—he skirted the edges of town in the quietest gear. The engine hardly made a noise, unlike the older models. Gust after gust of frigid air buffeted the snowmobile so much that he could barely hold it in a straight line. The town was so eerily dark, it reminded him of the tension he felt before a battle for a reason he could not explain. Luckily, Bishop wore a specialized helmet that lit up inside, played music, told him the temperature and wind speed, and gave directions. An additional feature of the helmet turned night into day with a built-in night vision option that turned off when there was any hint of artificial light so that the owner wouldn't be blinded.

As he rode through town, a white plastic grocery bag zipped through the air like a tiny parachute on a zip-line along with the snow that clouded his view. Once a dog skittered quickly past, its legs descending into the snow, and Bishop stopped to see where it went. But when he looked, the dog was gone; only his faint tracks remained.

Then his helmet switched off the night vision, alerting him of a vehicle approaching from the west. He turned quickly to a street on the right, and when he came to the next intersection, he took a left and switched a few more streets until he could view the vehicle from behind.

Two men drove a ski tractor and towed a trailer behind them piled high with boxes. Some of them were clear totes. He couldn't really tell from so far back what was in those totes, but he could guess. He followed at a distance until the truck pulled up in front of an old house. The tracks crunched on the top layer of snow. Bishop released the pressure on the throttle and watched from afar.

One driver stepped off the vehicle. His breath vapored behind him as he made his way through the snow and approached the front door of the house with his rifle at the ready. He pounded on the door with his gloved fist. He yelled, his voice cutting through the peace and quiet of the evening. "We know you're in there, Mr. Anderson." *Bam, bam, bam.* His fist pounded against the door as ice crystals, loosened by the vibration, fell from the roof and cascaded down around him, turning his snowsuit from gray to white.

"You're on the list, sir. Open the door." No one came. He flipped his wrist at the trailer, and another man hopped out of the back of the bed and sneaked around the back of the house. They'd obviously had a system to performing what looked to Bishop like nothing more than a raid.

In a second, Bishop saw a light flash up the inside of the house, and the front door opened soon afterward.

"Guy was hiding in the kitchen with a knife," said the man who'd sneaked around the back. He laughed.

"Hurry up," said the driver. "This is the last one for the night. It's too damn cold out here."

Soon, two other men jumped out of the truck, and three people were pulling items out of the house and tossing them into the back of the trailer with practiced ease while the lead guy kept watch outside. They'd been through this routine a few times before, it seemed.

Then a little old woman in a long, white, flowing nightgown came barreling out of the house screaming. She ran right up to the leader keeping watch and shouted in his face. "You might as well shoot us now! You killers!" He took the verbal onslaught for a while, and Bishop thought that would be it. It wasn't. The driver simply lifted his rifle and shot her once in the chest. She dropped down dead in front of him in a pile on the ice. The long fabric from her gown flapped in the wind. It was the callousness of the kill that shocked Bishop.

The driver then lit a cigarette and dropped the matchstick onto the woman's body. "Hurry up!" he yelled to the guys inside, who were running in and out of the house with armloads of food, clothing, blankets and gasoline.

Bishop had seen enough.

He put the snowmobile in gear, and driving with one arm he levered the other with his AR-15, and drove by slowly when he timed the other guys would be outside. He gunned them down. The three men never had a chance to raise their weapons before they were stitched with bullets across the chest and head.

Unfortunately, there was one person left in the house. He'd dropped a large bag of rice onto the snow before he fled back inside. The heavy bag sunk a foot into the snow on impact while he ran to take cover from Bishop's onslaught. Bishop stopped and waited in the silence for the man to come out again but only heard him make a radio call from within the house.

"Frank, we have a vigilante. Three down. Over…"

Aiming through a window, Bishop easily cut the man down where he hid inside.

"Done."

***

Bishop sped through the quiet streets. Every now and then he saw candlelight and a shadow behind it with a curtain draping back down into place quickly. There were people hidden in fear everywhere. Not only from the ice, but from this menace who had to go.

The police would be no help. If what he saw days ago was any indication, this group had already gained control of the town. He knew the best way to gain control himself was to cut off the head of the snake—and Frank Morton, he suspected, was the snake.

After Bishop had turned another corner, two sets of headlights turned on behind him. Finally they'd come out to play, and he was ready for them. He picked up speed and aimed to draw them farther out of town where he could deal with them more efficiently. The problem was the streets. The snow tractors couldn't keep up with his snowmobile. They were getting bogged down in the snow with increased speed, which forced Bishop to slow down. And they began firing on him in the street. Bishop didn't want to endanger the area residents, but *they* apparently didn't have any qualms about stray bullets taking out innocents.

Instead, Bishop turned a quick right behind another residential block, and in between houses he fired upon the first of his assailants. The driver veered, and the two guys standing in the back fell out onto the road along with several boxes of food. Bishop aimed and fired again, taking out two runners who'd taken off through the side yards of the houses. The second truck veered around the first and was coming up behind Bishop.

He threw a flash grenade and took off to distract them. Suddenly everything turned from night into day in a brief half second and then back again.

While the driver of the first snow tractor threw his arms over his head, the first truck recovered and backed up on the street, aiming to block Bishop on the road.

Bishop fired again, this time at the driver. The remaining guy in the back came out at him with his own illegal semiautomatic rifle. *I'll be damned,* Bishop thought. *I'm not the only one harboring illegal weapons.*

By this time, Bishop was blocked in on both sides of the narrow street. Not one to be intimidated, Bishop took the weakest route and shot down the man directly aiming at him. There were only two thugs left, and Bishop saw no need to let them live another day.

After pulling up behind the empty snow tractor, Bishop used it as coverage while he gunned down the other two men in a firefight that lasted all of five seconds. When both men dropped to the ground, again silence reigned.

The eerie quiet returned for more than a minute, and then a flicker caught his attention. Someone in the adjacent house had opened the door. The slender figure looked like it belonged to a young woman. She saw him standing there behind the truck and pointed to the food in the back of the sled trailer. He said nothing but watched as she ran into the street and grabbed a large bag lying there half-spilled. She picked it up and ran back into her house. Before he left, three more people, like ghosts, ran out as well and took what they could manage to recover and then fled again back into the darkness of their homes.

Bishop left then. He had to find a place to strike again. Taking them down one by one was the only way a single man could beat an army.

Chapter 34

"Who the hell is killing my men?" Frank demanded. He strangled the handheld radio, his blood pressure rising. "We already took care of the officers who didn't see things our way. Was there someone you missed?"

The police officer on the other end stuttered. "Frank, every...everyone here is on board. It's not one of us. Must be a resident. Over."

"Well, get down here and deal with him. There was only one witness that we found. Her tracks in the snow led us to her house. One man on a black snowmobile, full helmet—could be anyone. That's all she could tell us, anyway."

"All right. We'll go through town and see if anyone fits that description. There aren't that many people who are coming out of their houses let alone riding at night with their snowmobiles. I can't imagine who this could be. We've already taken possession of all working snow vehicles."

"Could this—I'm just saying—*could* this be one of your men?"

Frank was pissed at even the insinuation. His men were loyal: he'd made sure of that over the past few years. "Hell no! He gunned down four of my men. None of them would do that. Not unless they had a death wish or something. Get moving, Reuben."

"Yes, sir. Out."

"Cannot believe he would even suggest a thing like that. Cops..." Frank shook his head and smashed his cigarette butt out on a plate that Roman had handed him.

"We've got other problems," Roman said as he unbuttoned his suit jacket and sat at the head of the conference room table. With only him and Frank at the table, his voice seemed to boom off the walls of the spacious room. He turned his chair to the floor-to-ceiling window overlooking the frozen lake. "See those marks coming from across the bay?"

Frank stood and walked over to the window. The scene was unmistakable. A winter wonderland is what he saw, but as Roman warned him, the wonder was deceptive; these conditions were a kind of hell, and that was what he was looking at. Coming from the side of the lake were two unmistakable marks in the snow made by a sled tractor. "Yeah, I see them. Those are different than the ones we found by the massacre last night."

Roman nodded his head; his finger propped up his chin in thought. "Those are from the sheriff in Rockford Bay. He left us a note of his own last night. He says the people on the south side of the lake are starving. He wants food deliveries."

Frank chuckled. "Or what?"

"He didn't say."

"I see two sets of tracks out there. You let him go?"

Roman nodded. "I did. Let's see what he's got first. If we take him out now, he won't show his hand. His people are desperate. Desperate people do stupid things. There's no way they'll survive out there for long. I told him to bring his people in and we'd take care of them. He refused, of course."

"Are they armed?"

This time Roman chuckled. "Frank, everyone in Idaho is armed."

Frank put his hands on his hips and seemed transfixed by the scene beyond the window. "Still, I don't know. I've known the sheriff for a long time. He's a good man. He knows we killed off some of his officers because they wouldn't go along with things. We know he took some of his people with him when he left. He's not corruptible. He knew what he was doing. He knew he was beaten when all of this went down."

Roman nodded. "He did. He anticipated our move. The sheriff's a good leader. In time, he'll have to go. For now, let's see what he's got planned."

Frank stepped away from the window, breaking his trance on the winter scene. "Great, we've got a vigilante *and* a sheriff to deal with."

As Frank was leaving the office, Roman said, "Frank, they're both very dangerous. Don't underestimate either."

Frank paused at the heavy door and nodded with a grim but menacing expression.

Chapter 35

After returning to the storage unit, Bishop spent an additional hour covering his snow tracks in the early morning hours. The children were still asleep, and Maeve was relieved to see him. After she fell asleep, he bedded down near Jake and slept for a few hours until Jake began nibbling on his hair and tonguing his ear.

"Knock it off, you weirdo," he'd said and shoved his muzzle away. When he sat up, Maeve smiled at him and tried to suppress a laugh. Her hair was a fiery, wild, tangled mess. He'd never seen a lovelier sight.

He'd made it up to Jake later by rubbing him down and giving him feed and melted snow. His horse was like a good dog companion in many ways. He'd come when he whistled and demanded he pet him if he was nearby. Jake was like a big dumb Lab; he always seemed to sport a goofy grin and lolled around when he wasn't working.

"OK, you big goofball, that's all you're getting today. Stay out of trouble," he said. Again Bishop said goodbye to Maeve and the children before slipping out just before dawn.

Even dressed warmly, the temperature still seeped between the layers the instant Bishop went outside. Since it was near freezing inside the shelter, the temperature outside had to be closer to the single digits if not well below zero by now. This limited his activities, and if it limited his, it would also limit those of his enemies. Bishop would try to use that to his advantage, but unfortunately it meant that his adversaries would not come out to play where he could get to them without injuring innocent people. He'd have to go to them.

Starting where he'd last seen them, he intended to follow their tracks. Bishop raced over the snow to where he'd taken out the last of the looters. When he drove down that street with his night vision helmet activated, there was now only one body lying in the street, and it wasn't one of the guys he'd killed just a few hours before. The closer he came to the body, the worse the feeling in the pit of his stomach became.

When he was only three feet away, his pulse raged with hate. The one shadowy young woman who dared to run out for the fallen food lay dead. Her blond hair stained red, her white skin frozen in time—she'd been shot not once, but three times. Both of her thighs had gunshots through them, and the last one was through her temple. They'd tortured her. He guessed why. She'd seen him.

Bishop shook his head. "Condemn them to hell…" he said under his breath. Such a senseless killing. She probably had children in the home, he guessed. This had to stop. This had to stop now.

Bishop followed what looked like the tractor sled's distinguishing tracks. They were choppy on the outer sides and smooth on the inner, made by the larger tractor wheels in the front of the sled and the sleek blades of the vehicle carrying these sick bastards.

It didn't take long for Bishop to follow them far enough to see where they led. In fact, most of the tracks in the town were the same. Hardly anyone else traveled from their homes, even though occasional curtains flickered. He knew they were in there—just too afraid to come out.

An entire town was terrified because of the tyrant in the big hotel controlling everything.

Under cover of darkness, Bishop edged closer to the hotel, where the tracks had led him. They swung up into the parking garage multiple times. They were fresh, and Bishop wondered why they didn't try to hide them. Then he remembered the dead police officer on the lake and knew they didn't feel the need to cover their tracks. They owned the town now.

Hidden behind a corner building on East Front Avenue and Fourth Street, Bishop watched as guards walked back and forth in the opening of the parking garage attached to the hotel. Then something else caught his attention. A noise, and it sounded like its source was traveling closer, from across the south side of the lake. In his helmet, he used the magnify app and zeroed in on the source of the noise. There was a man on an older snowmobile. The louder gas two-stroke engine was from before everything became battery operated. Where the man got the gasoline mixture was a mystery to Bishop. With his night vision goggles, Bishop could only see that the traveler was alone and pulled a small trailer on skis behind his snowmobile. He wasn't certain if the guy was with the hotel bullies or not, but as the guards from the hotel scrambled to intercept him, he assumed the latter.

Afraid the guy was driving into his own death like the last guy he'd watched die on the ice, Bishop anticipated gunshots any minute. But that's not what happened. As the guards scrambled to intercept the guy, another man walked outside. This guy stood taller than rest. A few of the guards went to him for instruction, and he made hand gestures toward the guy on the ice. What surprised him was that it wasn't Frank. Nor were the men guarding the hotel Frank's men. These guys wore black uniforms, and Frank's men wore street clothes.

"Odd. This guy's got his own army."

Several of the uniformed hotel guards intercepted the guy on the ice. Or rather, they met him on the ice as he slowed down. Their rifles raised on his approach. The man, who held his hands up, didn't appear to be armed from Bishop's view and only talked to the men. One of the three guards stepped away and used his radio on his shoulder to relay what was probably a message. Bishop looked back at the parking garage and saw that two other guards were standing next to the leader, discussing something. Obviously they'd received the message and were contemplating what their next move would be. By this time, the sun was beginning to rise, and soon Bishop had to switch off the night vision to watch the scene unfold in front of him. Near dawn, some decision was made, and the three guards holding the traveler searched through his belongings and patted him down while another one held him at gunpoint. Whatever they were saying to the man, he seemed to object to it. He waved his arms angrily and made pleading gestures.

The three men then turned and began walking away from him as the traveler shouted at them. One of the guards turned back abruptly and yelled. This Bishop could hear from his position. "Do you want to die?" The guard aimed his rifle at the man's head. The traveler shook his head in defeat and turned on his engine, arching a circle with his vehicle and racing away the way he'd come.

Bishop didn't know the man, but he was obviously desperate. And from the previous scene here, he was surprised they let him live, let alone leave on his own.

Switching his view to the men standing in the opened parking garage, the taller man watched the traveler speed away. His breath clouded out behind him. He had to be freezing standing out there in only a coat, but it didn't seem to bother him. The guards left his side after saying something more, and the tall man stood there for a while longer, watching the ice. Then he turned and went back inside.

At that moment, Bishop knew who the enemy was. Frank was a henchman, but this guy was the head of the snake. The one Bishop needed to take down.

Bishop began to leave, but when he turned, he spotted someone coming around the back of the building where he was hiding. Immediately he knew he'd been too involved with what was going on in front of him so that he'd forgotten to check behind his position. The man was dressed in the black uniform associated with the guards of the hotel and was speaking rapidly into a mic on his shoulder while drawing a pistol from a holster on his side.

Bishop was already on his snowmobile, had started it, and was racing toward the guy, who aimed, fired, and missed as Bishop leaned to the side when he reached close proximity. Bishop kicked the guard square in the chest, flinging him into a snow berm. *Too late*, he thought. *They're on to me now*.

He took off up Fourth Street and jetted right onto East Indiana Avenue. Most of this was residential, and he couldn't leave tracks leading back to the storage unit, nor did he want to get anyone killed. When he hit Seventh Street, snow vehicles were coming from the south, so he made several shots in their direction.

He was desperately trying to get out of the residential streets when shots rang out behind him. He began zig-zagging in the street to evade the bullets and continued to gain distance. Nearing Phippeny Park on the right, Bishop swerved through the two-block-wide park, cutting between the trees until he sped east and then doubled back south on Eighth Street. If he could get them in between the streets, he could end this.

But by the time he hit Pennsylvania Avenue, sparks flew from a bullet hitting his engine cover. Someone was shooting at him from the west side. Continuing on in hopes of losing them, Bishop hit Foster Avenue but turned too late to see a roadblock pull into place, and not only that, but a young boy had emerged from his home between him and the roadblock and was walking out toward the road through the snow in his driveway.

Shots flew through the air, and all Bishop could think of in that split second was the child's life ending from a stray bullet. He was about three years old, dressed in head-to-foot pajamas. Beyond the boy, there were the men shooting at Bishop, heedless of the child making his way between them into the street. Bishop did the only thing he could think of, and that was intercepting the child. Bishop sped toward the enemy. Halfway there, he skidded down to the right, his kneecap grazing the ice as the boy entered the kill zone. He grabbed the child with his right arm as his snowmobile landed on its side between them and the enemy.

In seconds, the armed men were on them, shouting and pointing their weapons at him and the child. Bishop held his hands in the air in hopes they wouldn't kill the boy. The little boy cried out in fear. One of them grabbed the boy by the back of his pajamas and flung him away hard toward the path he came through in the snow.

Behind Bishop's helmet, he glared at the man. The child still screamed. Five armed men dressed in black quickly removed Bishop's helmet, knife and firearms and had fitted him with plasticuffs.

They roughly picked him up out of the snow and began leading him toward their vehicle. The child still screamed from where he'd landed. "Put the kid inside his house at least," Bishop shouted. They made no effort to do so.

Bishop struggled as they took him away, and one of the officers laughed and then took his rifle and butted Bishop in the side of the face. Blood spewed from Bishop's nose, and yet he yelled again, "You're going to kill him. Get the kid inside!" Again, the same officer this time raised his pistol and, before Bishop could duck, the handle end came crashing down against his skull. Bishop's vision faltered as his peripheral vision went black and what he could see was quickly zeroing out into darkness.

They didn't listen, and as they held Bishop down, the last thing he heard as he was losing consciousness was the sound of the boy's cries as he screamed from the snow berm beside the street.

In his last seconds of consciousness, his thoughts turned to another boy, Ben, and his mother and Louna, who were hiding still, hiding in a place they would not be safe in for long. Not from the men in his way, but from the greater danger, the cold.

Damn, I've killed us all.

Chapter 36

A child's cry was his last memory and was also what woke him as he lay on cold concrete floor. Groggily, Bishop realized the sound wasn't the cry of a child at all, but a thrumming in his head reminded him of what had happened.

He tried to rise, but as he lifted his cheek from the rough, cold floor, he found his hands were still tied behind his back.

He'd realized then, too, that he wasn't alone in the dark room. Someone else was in there with him and had made a noise like the brushing of fabric across the flooring, fibers catching on tiny concrete thorns.

"Who's there?"

Though no one answered, Bishop could hear him breathing in the dark. His breath was coming in and out in at a faster rate of speed, which meant he was scared. In Bishop's experience, scared men did dumb things. Things that got you killed despite the desire to save yourself. Like he did earlier, trying to save the child from the crossfire only for the little boy to freeze to death in the snowbank where the thugs had left him.

Attempting to sit up, Bishop rolled over first onto his side and then scooted backward a few feet until he hit a wall. He leaned against the solid structure and felt grooves in the wall with his fingers. A painted cinderblock wall was easy to detect. *Must be in the building's basement.*

"Hey," he called out to the unseen occupant. His voice bounced off the walls. *The ceiling must be high in here. Maybe a stairwell?*

He tried again. "Hey, I know you're there. I can hear you." He didn't hear anything for a second, only another shift of fabric on the floor. "Hey, what's your name?"

Silence for a time and then, "I'm…Austin. Austin Sanchez."

Young man, Bishop thought at the sound of his voice. *Not more than twenty-five.*

"Why are you here, Austin?"

"I…I won't do what Roman wants me to do. I'm Mr. Geller's personal assistant. I'm not a…a gangster."

"Who's Mr. Geller?

He laughed, incredulous. "Mr. Geller owns this hotel and half the town."

"Where is he now?"

"He flew back to Arizona. He doesn't know any of this is going on. He wouldn't allow it. Mr. Geller is a good man."

Bishop nodded in the dark. Pieces of the puzzle were starting to fall into place. "Who's running the show now?"

"His name is Roman. He's Mr. Geller's manager."

Bishop thought about this for a moment. "Roman a tall guy? Dark hair?"

"Yeah."

"Do you have any way of contacting Mr. Geller?"

Austin sighed. "No, cell towers are down. I don't even know if he made it there. I hope he did. They took me prisoner right after he left."

"How often do they come to check on you?"

"Twice a day," he said, his voice back to normal. However, it was so cold in the room that Bishop knew if they were left there without heat, they'd die of exposure in a matter of days.

"Each time they come in, it's the same thing. They ask if I'll join them. They say I only have one day left to decide."

"Join what?"

"I guess, join them. I don't understand why they haven't killed me yet. They've already killed so many."

"Does Roman come here himself?"

"No, I last saw him right after Mr. Geller left on the helipad. That was like a week ago. Right before this all began."

Hmmm. The question that had plagued Austin now plagued Bishop. Why hadn't they killed him long ago? There had to be a reason, since killing seemed so easy to them. These men who abandon children to die weren't likely to think twice about offing someone who wouldn't go along with their plans. There must be something special about Austin, or there was the possibility that he was lying to Bishop. The thought crossed his mind. Possibly he had been stowed there to gain information about Bishop, the vigilante who came to take the town.

Before he could ask questions, though, the door opened. As it did, a stream of light spiked into the room and separated shadows on the floor that rose up the wall and instantly confirmed Bishop's guess that he was in the bottom of a concrete stairwell.

Besides the light, a rifle appeared in the doorway, followed by three men all dressed in black, and then the light source appeared in the form of an electric lantern.

"Hello," the first guard said as he shined the light onto Bishop. Even though he knew it might be a waste of effort, his hands worked overtime in trying to free themselves from the plasticuffs behind his back.

"What's your name, sir?"

Bishop diverted his eyes to the young man sitting across from him. He had a blanket wrapped around his shoulders. His blond hair was mussed, and the first thing Bishop zeroed in on was the bruising around his right eye. Someone had roughed him up. His shirtsleeve was torn, and there was old dried blood on the kid's shirt. He was thin and, worse yet, had the look of someone defeated. He made eye contact with Bishop for a second before looking down again. In that short time, Bishop didn't think the kid was a spy, but he was no expert on human behavior. That young man was in pain and, judging by his defensive stance, he didn't trust the guards to not hurt him again.

"What do you want?" Bishop asked, ignoring the question, swinging his attention directly to the closest guard at the same time he secretly wrestled with freeing himself of the restraints.

The guard stepped aside and let another man into the room. A man Bishop had seen before in town and kept his distance from. Frank moved toward him with a grin on his face and a cigarette between his lips. Dressed in denim and snow boots, he didn't have the swagger he usually walked with, but he was menacing all the same.

"I know you," Frank said, pointing his cigarette at him. He flicked his ashes on Bishop's black pants. The red glow within the ashes threatened to burn a hole in the nylon snow gear. Bishop brushed it off with his other leg before it got the chance.

"You're that guy." Frank said it in such a way that Bishop wasn't sure if he really knew who he was at all. He was only taking a stab in the dark about his identity. Bishop had only run into Frank once, but it was a memorable event and one that Bishop never intended to repeat again.

The man scrunched his brows together for a moment as if that would jar his memory. "I know I've seen you before. But it doesn't matter now because you're a dead man anyway."

"Tell me something I don't already know, you coward."

Frank's laughter bounced off the concrete walls. "Dead man's funny," he said the guard next to him. "It doesn't matter who you are. You don't exist beyond this room and you never will again."

Frank abruptly averted his attention away from Bishop and addressed Austin.

"Last chance, son. This is it. You have to join us. Roman said so."

Austin squirmed in his seat. He looked terrified. His gaze went from Frank to Bishop, pleading for help, but there was nothing Bishop could do. "I...I can't do what they do. I won't."

Frank knelt at the young man's side. "Look, kid. You're going to *die* unless you do this. I can't step in anymore."

Bishop watched the exchange, and it appeared to him that Frank genuinely cared for the kid. He was almost pleading with him.

"Just go along, Austin. I'll make sure you're with good people. I'll look out for you."

Austin searched Frank's face. He was nearly in tears. "But why?"

Frank rubbed his eyes and shook his head. "I made a promise to your mother a long time ago. I intend to keep it. Look, I'll make sure you're out of the way of things. OK? Just say you'll go along."

Austin again looked to Bishop as if he would have the answers.

Frank tapped him on the leg again. "Hey, I need an answer now."

Austin nodded tentatively at first and then said, "OK."

"That's a good lad," Frank said and helped Austin stand. He removed his cuffs while he said, "You have to do one thing first before you can leave this room, though. You have to prove yourself, Austin. This one time. I won't ask you to do it again. But this time, you have to do it. Understand?"

"Do what?" Austin asked, surprised, but Bishop had a sick feeling he knew what the task would be.

When Frank pulled a gleaming .50 Cal Desert Eagle out of his shoulder holster, that he kept on at all times without regard to concealment, and put the heavy, chrome gun in Austin's hands, Bishop knew his hunch was right.

Frank pointed to Bishop on the floor. "Kill him."

Austin jerked and shook his head quickly. "I…I can't. I said I wouldn't do anything like that."

Frank put his hands on both of Austin's arms. "Just this one time. That's all it will take for you prove yourself. Just shoot him once in the chest. That's all you have to do. That's the only way you're leaving this room."

Frank motioned for the guards to leave. "I'll stand right outside the door, Austin. You can't miss. Just one shot to the chest. That's all I ask."

As soon as the door shut, Bishop levered his eyes at him and worked his muscles overtime to shed the cuffs as he said, "Kid, you shoot that Desert Eagle in here against these concrete walls and the bullet will ricochet. You're likely to hit yourself in this close proximity. I'm just warning you."

"I'm sorry. I don't want to do this. I don't have a choice," Austin said, his hands shaking rapidly. "I'm sorry," he said again and began to aim the heavy pistol in Bishop's general direction. The muzzle shook terribly.

"You don't have to do this, Austin. They're trying to control you. Trying to make you a murderer. Don't let them. If you kill me, others will die."

"They're going to kill you anyway."

With the cuffs burning hot with friction and tension, Bishop bought more time by saying, "You don't have to be the one doing the killing. There has to be some reason they haven't already taken you out. Why do they want to keep you alive? Who are you?"

"I know what the reason is," Austin said, crying.

"What?"

Shaking his head, Austin said quietly, "I'm his son. I'm Mr. Geller's biological son. No one knows but a few people. Mr. Geller doesn't even know that I know."

"Then you're worth more to them alive than dead. Don't let them do this to you, Austin. Your father would expect more from you."

At that moment, Austin's aim faltered. He nearly had his eyes closed by then. His finger within the trigger guard, Austin was going to fire, and by Bishop's estimation, he was going to miss and likely kill himself in the process. With a last surge of strength, one cuff popped free. Quickly launching his leg out, Bishop knocked Austin's feet from underneath him and, using his freed hands, quickly grabbed the gun and fired once, straight up in the air at the angle of the ascending stairs. Then Bishop immediately dropped the magazine and found it full having shot the one in the chamber. "Seven bullets left."

Opening the door, Frank was met with a direct shot to the face, and three more shots were fired in quick succession into the center mass of the three guards before they even had a chance to ready their weapons. In practice, Bishop would have preferred double tapping them, but there was little time for the best-case scenario and he knew the Desert Eagle rounds did a sufficient job on their own. Now he only held three.

He quickly stepped over Frank's body and grabbed the AR-15 rifles from the three guards, then an additional weapon from Frank's body along with all the keycards or IDs the four men had in their possession. He turned handing one of the rifles to see Austin standing behind him with a blank look and his mouth agape. "Come on, kid, we've got to run."

"I was…I was going to shoot you."

"But you didn't. Come on, we don't have time for this now." He grabbed at Austin's sleeve and guided him over the bodies. "How do we get out of here?"

"Up and to the left. There's a door to the lobby."

A crackle from a radio sounded. "Boss, you there? Over."

"Come on," Bishop said gruffly. "We have to find a place to hide out. I need you to help me find Roman."

The kid was hesitant. He stood perfectly still. Bishop watched his eyes dart back and forth as if he was flipping through the many options available to him and coming up empty. He wanted to flee, that much was clear, but Bishop needed him, needed his guidance to traverse the building and to point out the bad guys. He needed Austin to tell him who to kill. And he needed him to do it now.

"Kid, we don't have time for this. Your dad would want you to help me."

Austin met his eyes finally. Maybe that was enough to convince him, but Bishop wasn't sure.

"He'll be in the penthouse this time of day," Austin said. "This way. Up the stairs." Austin rushed past Bishop, but the older man caught him by the arm. "You need to let me lead. Here," he said and handed him one of the rifles. "Don't put your finger in there unless you're going to shoot."

"I know. Mr. Geller taught me," Austin said, and Bishop led the way up the stairwell with his new guide, thinking, *At least the old man had done that much for the kid.*

Chapter 37

Frozen in fear, Maeve held her finger to her lips as her son and Louna stared back at her with frightened eyes.

Crunch...crunch...crunch...

Jake chose that moment to swing his tail. The slight sound of his tail hitting the plastic of a nearby box made her cringe. The enigma of an environment covered with snow in a freezing world was the amplification of sound. As if everything were covered in a warm comfy blanket, even a needle dropped on a concrete floor pinged its way to one's eardrums—distinctive and sure.

Half-tempted to go and still Jake's tail, she didn't dare move for fear of the fibers in her clothing rubbing together. Or the sounds of her light steps against the flooring.

In the meantime, the footsteps outside the storage unit were nearing, growing louder and louder in intervals. With her Glock out in front of her and the children behind her, Maeve shivered more out of fear than the cold.

Whoever it was stopped right outside the metal door. Bargaining with herself, she made a few internal rules. *If he knocks, I won't say a thing. If he tries to get inside, I'll shoot. He has to attempt to enter, and then I'll shoot, but not before.*

Glancing back at the children, their wide eyes round in fear, she swallowed and turned her attention back to the door. Her breath came out in rapid puffs of vapor.

Another crunch in the snow. And then another. One more, and then soon she heard the steps of whoever had come retreat until she heard them no more.

Chapter 38

"We have to go through the lobby to get to the next stairwell. It's near the elevators that lead up to the penthouse."

"How likely is it those guards of his will be out there? Is there surveillance?"

Austin shook his head no. "The power's out. They lost that capability. I don't know about the guards."

"Don't they have generators going?"

"I really don't know."

"Well, we're about to find out." Bishop opened the door a crack. What he saw startled him, but it was what he felt that confused him more. Waves of comforting heat poured into the frigid crack in the doorway. He stared at an enormous raging fireplace with not one person around to enjoy it—as far as he could tell from his limited view of the lobby. Though if someone were, he'd be nice and toasty.

From his limited boyhood memories from when he'd visited the grand hotel with his family, Bishop remembered the lobby being enormous. But he was a boy then, and it had seemed to take them forever to walk from one end to the other where the hotel restaurant stood. Listening for any sign of another person, he searched for the other stairwell Austin had mentioned. Across the hallway, near the elevators, stood a door with a familiar plaque to the side of it. He turned back to Austin and motioned for him to follow.

They sneaked out quickly, and Bishop covered Austin as he scrambled across the hallway. He almost hated leaving the warmth of the lobby for the frigid cold of the next stairwell, but it must be done. He imagined inviting the town in there and letting them enjoy the warmth for the first time in weeks instead of the frozen cold.

Inside the next stairwell, it didn't take long for them to see their own breaths again. Bishop made sure the coast was clear before proceeding. "How the heck are they getting up and down fifteen floors without the elevators working and without using the stairs?"

"Roman had most of the guests leave before the weather became too bad for them to go. He basically threw them out into the cold. Most of the service people are staying up top on the restaurant floor, and they take the service entry up and down most of the time. It's an elevator that runs on less power. The generator could run it, but there's also another set of stairs for the staff, so I imagine they use those."

"I see. So we're unlikely to meet anyone as we come up and down the main stairwell?"

Austin hunched his shoulders. "We might run into a guest or two. They're not aware of the service entry. A few of them stayed, but no one is caring for them."

Stopping on the darkened stairs, Bishop turned to shine his light on Austin. "So, they hear the gunshots and see what's going on from their hotel rooms, and they're terrified, basically?"

"I imagine so."

"*That's* hospitality," he said and continued on until they reached the fifth floor in the dark. Their breaths were becoming more winded with each step when he turned to look at Austin, who had fallen a little behind. "You OK?"

"Yeah…I usually take the elevator, *hah*."

Then a sudden *clang* from above caused Bishop to shift his weapon and raise his hand to halt Austin's movements.

A sudden globe of light flashed on the concrete wall, and then came the descending sound of feet quickly traversing steps. Austin's eyes became as large as saucers, and he shifted in an attempt to run downward when Bishop caught him by the back of his shirt, stopping him abruptly.

Signaling with his finger to his lips, Bishop then pointed to the corner in the lower stairwell and moved his hand up and down in a "lay low" gesture. After releasing Austin's shirt, he watched as the young man quietly went to the spot that Bishop suggested. The main task for him was to urge the boy not to panic. Panicking would get them both killed. As Austin retreated, Bishop ascended the stairs toward the danger and watched as the globe of light on the wall bounced with each step and traveled ever closer. Bishop remained in the shadow of the light, and as soon as the owner came into view, Bishop let his finger enter the trigger guard of his rifle. He began to squeeze when suddenly, instead of the man coming to the next floor and to his imminent death, the stranger shifted and opened the door to the floor right above Bishop's position.

His finger released the pressure on the trigger, and he removed it from the guard. Bishop's breath returned to normal as the door clanged shut, but before it did, he heard voices from the other side.

Shining his light on Austin below, he waved for him to come up to his position. They were passing the door where the intruder exited only to come face to face with another guard when the door suddenly opened again.

Dumbfounded, the guard dressed in black still had his rifle slung over his back. A long blue-carpeted hallway extended behind him, and another guard was walking away so that Bishop could barely see his back. Quickly he grabbed the guard in front of him, his hand wrapped around his mouth, and pulled him around to his chest to keep him from reaching for his weapon. Austin stumbled backward as Bishop pulled the guard through the darkened doorway and let the door close with a *click*.

Inside the darkness, Bishop had no choice—any struggle from the man would alert the rest to their position. Releasing his hand from the guard's mouth, he extended his reach around his head and twisted with a sudden jerk. The man fell to his feet.

Austin met his eyes, and the boy was in utter fear.

"I had to, Austin. He would have exposed us. We need to get to Roman, quickly. The stairs are taking too long. Where's the nearest elevator?"

Austin still frozen in terror, Bishop knew this was too much for the kid. "Austin, quickly. I'm trying to keep you alive."

Austin pointed to the door from which the guard had just come.

"All right, come on. Whatever happens, stay right behind me. If you're not there, I can't help you. Understand?"

He nodded.

"Let's go."

"I'm scared," Austin quickly uttered.

Turning to the boy, Bishop whispered, "The only way out is through. Say it."

"The...only way out is through," Austin repeated.

"Say it over and over in your mind. The only way out is through. Let's go now."

The younger man's breath slowed a bit, and Bishop knew Austin was doing as he had as a young man in war, repeating that same mantra over and over in his mind. *The only way out is through. The only way out is through. The only way out is through.*

Chapter 39

A few hours later, Maeve dozed while the children slept as they waited for Bishop. A sudden sound of gushing water woke her, and when she jerked her head around to see where it was coming from, the smell hit her too. Standing at the side end of the storage unit, Jake had just let go of his water. Horse urine had a distinctive smell, and Louna popped her head out from the covers, staring at her with her nose pinched.

There was nothing she could do about the situation. They were trapped inside with Jake. She should have known something like this was going to happen because for the past hour Jake had seemed agitated. He'd probably had needed to go for a while but didn't want to do it in his own space but finally had no choice. Large puddles of yellow liquid began to pool and seep toward the unit door with the slight slope of the concrete.

"Ah, Mom!" Ben said.

"Shh! We can't make any noise or those people might come back."

Ben nodded his head then covered his nose with the blanket.

How much longer can we live this way? she thought. *As long as it takes* was her sudden reply to herself.

"At least it's draining away," she whispered to the children.

Ben only nodded.

For the first time in her life, she found herself wondering at what temperature a horse's urine would freeze. *There's got to be a lot of salt in that, I guess?*

Crunch...crunch...crunch.

Maeve crouched low and held her hand out to the children, motioning them to keep quiet. Whoever had come before was back again. And then, bwaa, bwaa, bwaa...bwaa, bwaa, bwaa...A tremendously loud alarm sounded in the distance.

The footsteps stopped as the alarm continued, and then they pounded on quickly, this time stopping right outside the storage unit. *Bam, bam, bam.*

Her breaths coming in a rapid staccato, Maeve held her rifle out in front of her.

"I know you're in there. Open the damn door!"

Out of the corner of her vision, she saw her son stand. She turned to him and shook her head. Tears coming down her face, she kept her aim on the invisible man on the other side of the metal door. He pounded again and again. "Open this door!" he growled.

The muzzle of the Glock shook in her hands. *If he comes inside, I'll shoot.*

The scratch of metal on metal began as he pulled up on the door. Slivers of light flashed inside. The door jerked up and down.

If he comes inside, I'll shoot...

Chapter 40

Running through the hallway with emergency lights as the only illumination, Bishop and Austin made it halfway down when suddenly the alarm system went off. Now the dim lights flashed as well. They could hear running footsteps down the other side of the hall. Black suits flashed by without any heed to them coming toward them.

They must have found the bodies in the basement.

Chaos was good. Bishop would use it to his advantage. When one of the black suits saw them from down the hallway, his eyes first shifted to Bishop's rifle, and then he made eye contact with Bishop while lifting his weapon. Bishop stopped and kicked open one of the hotel room doors, flinging the kid inside from behind while he aimed and fired at the guy. Bishop watched as he hit the ground but the commotion attracted others, he followed Austin into the darkened hotel room and used the doorway as cover as he stitched the next guard across the chest with three shots.

He could see the elevator at the end of the hall from his position, and they only needed to make it there to get to the floors above.

"Come on," Bishop said and had to pull Austin by his arm to the hallway. When they passed the downed guard, Bishop stopped and picked up his gun.

"You'll need his badge to the get to the top floor," Austin said, and there tethered to the front of the guard's jacket was the badge Austin mentioned. He reached down and snapped it off. They stopped again at the end of the hallway. The downed guard was the last to cross, and in the corridor the alarm squalled to the point that Bishop wanted to cover his ears. Austin pressed the elevator door's button to go up, and they waited. Another hallway attached here that went the opposite direction, and Austin's eyes darted from one to the other. They had no idea if anyone else was coming. When the elevator's floor indicator light neared their level, Bishop pulled Austin behind him and aimed at the opening elevator car. The doors opened, and thankfully, they found the space empty.

Inside, Austin took the card from Bishop and flashed it at the unit on the control panel, then pressed the button for the penthouse suite where Roman stayed. Before the elevator door closed, though, Bishop raised his rifle once again as he saw two figures enter the hallway. The elderly man and his wife's shocked expressions were all he saw in the split second before the door closed. There were innocent people here, and he would do everything he could to avoid harming them in the process of getting rid of the plague known as Roman.

Keeping to the side of the car with Austin positioned behind him, the elevator rose and then stopped with a *ding*. The doors opened slightly and then all at once to an opulent room filled with warmth and fur rugs strewn across white stone floors approaching a desk flanked by leather couches. Heat emanated from a fireplace much like the one in the lobby but much smaller.

Creeping out of the elevator, Bishop practically dragged Austin behind him. He let go of the boy's shirtsleeve when a door slammed. Suddenly the alarm stopped, but his ears continued to ring. Bishop scanned the room and looked down the hallway where he'd heard the noise. He motioned his head toward the hall with a questioning look, and Austin nodded that he had the right idea.

He tapped Austin on the chest and pointed to a tall white reception desk. The boy was more of a hindrance than a help, and he needed to stash him in a safe place out of the way.

Austin nodded, only too thankful to comply. He scurried behind the high white desk and hid down low.

Bishop waited until the young man was out of sight before he continued onward. Sudden dim light filled the hallway to the left, and when Bishop looked he found that the left side of the hallway was opened to windows that were letting what light there was seep through. He was utterly exposed there at fifteen floors up, and when he looked out the windows, he saw men in black running around in all directions on the ground below. They were looking high and low for them outside in the frozen landscape, but not high enough.

They assumed he and Austin had fled outside, and why not? They'd never expected someone to head toward danger.

A distinctive clicking sound, one Bishop was all too familiar with, came from the other side of the door, commanding his attention from the scene outside the windows. Whoever was on the other side of that door knew there was danger near.

Hurrying to the edge of the heavy closed door, Bishop waited and listened. As a shadow blocked the sliver of light from coming underneath the doorway, Bishop watched as the silver door handle began to twist.

Chapter 41

Metal snapped, something heavy clanged to the ground, and the door whipped upward, all at once flashing light inside. Maeve was blinded. Her first instinct was to shield her eyes with her left hand. She caught herself as a man stepped inside. He held a rifle pointed at her and the children behind her and yelled roughly, "Put it down."

For a second, she had no idea what he was talking about and then remembered she was holding him at gunpoint. With a menacing look, he glanced behind her at the children and then to the side, at the horse. After a moment, he sniffed the air. "You piss your pants?" he yelled at the children.

No one answered him, and he didn't seem to expect an answer as his eyes were too busy plundering the boxes behind the children. Whatever was in those boxes, he wanted to know.

"I found your tracks outside. Whoever tried to hide them thought he was clever. Stand up and put your damn gun down *now*, or I'll shoot you. I don't give a damn about kids either."

She believed him and silently screamed at herself as she found she was lowering her own weapon in defeat. There was no way she could endanger the children. Knowing Bishop would be disappointed, she did as he warned against. *You're making a mistake*, she screamed to herself. *Shoot him!*

"Geez, you're a pretty thing. You'll fetch a nice price."

Boom!

Maeve ducked, and the tremendous noise came from behind her. Her hands were in the air when she turned to her children to protect them from the unknown shooter. Then she saw her son standing there.

A small swirl of smoke whirled up from the muzzle end of his rifle. Her son Ben stood there, his eyes locked on the downed man in front of them, his mouth slightly agape.

"Ben!"

She went to comfort her son when the man on the ground began to move. Twisting, Maeve launched herself to her Ruger and raised the weapon just in time to pull the trigger before the assailant wrapped his hand around the hilt of his own.

This time, she knew for certain he was done for. Half of the man's head sprayed across the concrete ground and into the snow, the crimson and gray in bright contrast to the bright white snowflakes coming down.

Chapter 42

Now, slowly, with a creak of its hinges, the heavy wooden door moved. It crept open, exposing the muzzle end of an AR-15; then, with the sound of friction of metal against the edge of wood, more of the weapon appeared.

Stiff-lipped, Bishop leaned against the wall, slid his hand into his holster, and pulled out the handgun without a sound. Then he pulled his right leg upward and kicked at the door all at once.

A shot fired from the rifle, shattering the hallway of windows. Subzero wind flooded the interior; white, billowy curtains flapped out in the sudden breeze. The owner of the rifle attempted to pull the muzzle free by yanking it inside, but Bishop had it trapped.

He fired once through the wood of the door at chest height. Wood fragments blasted all over. The rifle slackened, and the barrel end bent downward. For a brief second, Bishop thought that was the end…thought he'd killed the guy on the other side, but he was mistaken.

A body slammed into the door. The force of it knocked Bishop's leg away, and the knob slammed into his gut. The Desert Eagle in his right hand was trapped in the corner, disabling him from bringing it upward. The door opened again, only to knock into him once more with full force. This time, there were hands gripping the edge of the heavy door. The rifle had fallen to the ground.

Bishop shoved his boot outward to stop the door from nailing him a third time, reached around with his left arm, and grabbed the assailant by the waist.

When he finally laid eyes on the man, he had no doubt in the brief nanosecond their eyes met that it was Roman. Tall guy, dark hair, but most of all, a menacing grin. He was enjoying this.

Shattered glass and air gusted inside as the two men struggled. The floor-to-ceiling windows were practically gone as Bishop wrangled the man into the precarious hallway that had suddenly become a fifteen-story cliff.

The rifle Roman dropped to the ground among the glass shifted on the floor as they struggled. Roman reached for the gun, but Bishop kicked it away just in time and out into the opened chasm of shattered glass. Briefly in midair, the rifle sailed downward and out of sight.

Struggling to point the gleaming Desert Eagle, Roman held Bishop's arm upward, and strength against strength, they wrestled. The man had more than five inches on Bishop in height. And not knowing exactly how it happened, they were on the shattered glass–strewn floor. Bishop's back pressed against the sharp fragments. Roman slammed Bishop's right arm again and again against the ground, but even though pain shot through his injured shoulder, he wasn't giving up the weapon in his grasp no matter what Roman tried to do.

Then Roman seemed to have a new tactic. He looked out the shattered window and began sliding Bishop's body with furious tugs toward the abyss. Bishop's boots soon were in free space and dangling fifteen stories above the ground. He would soon have to make a choice: to loosen his grip on Roman and grab onto something or he was done for.

Finally, Bishop threw his own forehead upward, slamming into Roman's head and stunning him briefly. Just enough for him to loosen his grip on Bishop's arm. With just enough time to raise the handgun, Bishop fired into the man's chest once, but Roman twisted at the last second and only shrapnel from the floor shot everywhere. He let go of Roman's arm with his left hand and punched the bigger man in the jaw, but Roman wasn't done yet.

Knowing he had only one bullet left in the gun, he continued to fight. Roman clawed for Bishop and shoved him even further over the edge. With his ass halfway over the ledge, Bishop raised the gun once more and sent the last round right into Roman's chest, but at a price. Bishop dropped the spent gun and dangled dangerously over the edge with Roman's body over his chest and began to lose his fight with gravity as he tried to scramble back over, only to catch shards of glass with his hands. About to panic in the inevitable freefall to his own death, another hand reached out and grabbed him by his jacket and hauled him back to safety.

Breathing hard, with blood mixed with the glass impaled in his hands, Bishop looked up to see Austin and said with heaving breaths of air, "Thanks, man. Just…in…time."

Chapter 43

Tentatively, Maeve took steps toward the torn menace of the man crumpled in front of her.

"Careful, Mom!" Ben warned from behind her.

"Stay where you are," she said to her son. With her eyes, she saw only blood, bone, and brain. And before she could kick at his body and close the door, her stomach dry heaved against her will. She knelt over to the side, involuntarily lurching. Not even looking, all she saw in her mind was the gray matter mixed with blood. Blood she spilled to save her son. The overwhelming nausea seemed like it would never subside, but finally it did. She wiped the thick saliva from her lips and stood once again.

The little girl was crying great sobs with her head buried in the blankets. Her son stood in shock, still holding on to his rifle in his hands.

A noxious mixture of strong urine, iron, and bile made her decide. She found herself leading Jake out of the storage unit just ten feet into the snow-covered alleyway. His gentle eyes looked at her as if nothing terrible had happened. She tied his lead to another unit's door lock and then came to the dead man in her way.

She avoided looking at the mangled part of him and kept her vision to his feet. She kicked away his gun in the snow and then straightened his legs out in front of him. Pulling his legs to the side, she dragged the man five feet with all the strength she had. Dropping his feet finally into the snow, she returned to the unit and looked for a shovel.

Needing to remove the rest of him that remained, Maeve looked along the walls until she spotted a long-handled shovel among the other tools. She didn't want to look at the bits of him that were still out there out of fear she'd have to vomit again.

After taking a couple of deep breaths, Maeve took another look at the kids. Louna still sobbing, her son patted the girl on the back but still clutched his rifle. With resolve, she turned and slid the blade of the shovel under the largest bloody chunks and walked a few paces with the offensive load and dumped it on the guy's chest. Returning for another load, she scraped the ice on the pavement outside the unit for as long as she could manage and dumped that load on its owner too as if to say, "Here you go. This belongs to you."

Then she shoveled snow over the man until he was a mound against a berm. She packed more snow over the last scattering marks of blood in the snow near the entrance to their unit. The whole time, the plummeting temperatures continued to seep through her and steal her inner heat. She was shaking before long. Her hands trembled as she carried the shovel and what dim light there was began to darken.

"Where is Bishop?" she wondered out loud and stared blankly toward where the alarms had been coming from before.

"Mom?"

Maeve turned to her son. "We should bring Jake back inside and close the door."

Nodding to herself, she first brought in a few shovelfuls of clean snow, dumped them at the high point of where Jake left his mess, and scooted the snow in a downward motion toward the end of the concrete, shoveling some of the urine out with it.

Then she retrieved Jake and put him back in his spot. Looking at the trampled snow, she used the back of the shovel to try and level the evidence of them being there and to mask the steps, but eventually she could see it was no use. Anyone coming this way would know there was someone there. Before she closed the door, she gazed at the mound with the dead man beneath. The first person she'd ever killed, the one who nearly killed them. Quietly she lowered the metal door the rest of the way, hoping no one could hear them, and she wondered if Bishop's life had also ceased with the end of the alarms from earlier.

Chapter 44

"He nearly shoved you out," Austin said, his eyes round.

"Yeah, he did at that." Bishop pointed at the body. "Was that Roman?"

Austin nodded his head. "Yes, that was him."

"That's a relief. I don't want to go through that again today." He was still trying to catch his breath. "Guy was relentless. Nearly killed me."

Holding on to the edge of the wall with a firm grip, Bishop leaned outward and looked below. Men in black were still wandering around looking for the enemy.

"Who are those guys?" Bishop gestured with his chin.

Austin laughed. "They're hotel security and bellboys and staff."

"Did they like this guy much?"

"No one liked Roman."

"So, you don't think they'll miss him?"

"That, I don't know. They did what he said without question. If they didn't, they were dead men."

"Well, let's send them a message," Bishop said and pushed Roman's body over the edge where the man had attempted to send him earlier.

Now, in silent descent, the black-suited dead man tumbled through the vast empty space; his suit jacket flapped in the wind, and then, with an audible thud, the body hit the snowy ground and caught the attention of all those on watch.

Observing, Bishop leaned out the window farther, gusts of wind drying his eyes. Three armed men approached the body, then stood again and looked up. While one returned quickly inside the building with his rifle jangling behind him, the other two wandered away, leaving abandoned footsteps in their wake.

"Let's get down there and see where we're at. Same rules as before—stay close behind me."

Austin nodded. "The only way out is through."

"Yeah," Bishop said and exited the penthouse. They hit the elevator down button and waited cautiously. Soon the car opened, and once inside, Bishop hit the lobby button.

"You sure?" Austin asked with concern.

"I have a hunch we're done here, but if we have any issues, follow my lead."

Descending the fifteen floors took too much time for Bishop to think. He'd been away from Maeve too long, and he pictured them huddled in the dark, worried and scared while they waited for his return.

Suddenly, the elevator door opened. Bishop craned his head around the corner to sneak a peek into the lobby, where he saw several men dressed in black standing in front of the raging fireplace facing him.

No one said a word. On the ground in front of them was a pile of rifles. Bishop looked from one face to another and said to Austin, "They're all boys. Not one over twenty-five."

"Roman made sure anyone who went against him died. The older men were the first to go."

Tentatively, Bishop stepped out of the elevator. "Raise your hands where I can see them," he yelled loud and clear.

One step after the other, Bishop kept his rifle trained for any sudden movement. There were at least twenty young men standing in the lobby. Most of them bore looks of shame; some of them even cried.

Bishop used that to his advantage. With a commanding voice, he yelled, "Take off your black shirts and your black pants now. Any sudden movement and you all die."

They looked from one to the other, and slowly they did as Bishop demanded. Soon the young men stood in their underwear. Some wore boxers while a few wore briefs.

As Austin watched his back, Bishop motioned his rifle at a smaller man on the left. "You. Pick up the clothes and toss them into the fireplace."

The scared boy nodded and did as Bishop said.

Sparks flew out as he hefted the load inside. The enormous fireplace *whooshed* with a fresh blaze.

"That's it. You." He pointed to a taller kid. "Are there any more of you anywhere?"

"No sir!" he said at first and then looked around. "Well, a few left already."

"Where did they go?"

The kid looked around. "*Home*, sir?" His statement came out more like a guess.

Bishop looked at their young faces again. "You damn stupid kids!" He couldn't just let them go. They were murderers and thieves. They were the minions of a tyrant much like the soldiers that served the horrors of Hitler.

"You don't blindly follow anyone! Use your damn brains!"

His angry voice rattled them. Each of them took steps backward in nervous fright. He had to do something. The people in the town were terrified and dying because of them. Because of Roman's demands, but ultimately because these boys gave Roman that power by following his orders and complying with his requests without questioning authority.

"Never will you wear that uniform again. Is that understood?" he bellowed.

"Yes, sir."

"That uniform is what terrified these people now. You've succeeded in ingraining that terror into them. They're dying out there. Your families, remember them? The people you've abandoned? That uniform is no different than a swastika. If I see anyone wear it again, they're dead. Is that clear?"

"Yes, sir!" they said in unison, more loudly this time.

"All of you…leave. Just as you are. In your shoes and underwear. Go to your homes and beg forgiveness from your loved ones if you have them. If you don't have a home here, you'll have to beg entrance somewhere else. Some of you will die in your attempt for salvation, but that's the price you paid. You're at the mercy of these people now."

Again they each looked to one another, and when no clear leader emerged, one of them edged toward the door, as if uncertain they were really free to go. They all went as a group. Some of them ran immediately in no particular direction. Some followed others. With the weather well below freezing, they wouldn't get very far.

Chapter 45

Opening the door, Bishop began to walk out.

"Where are you going?" Austin asked. "You can't just leave now!"

Putting a hand on Austin's shoulder, Bishop asked, "Is there an intercom in the building?"

"Yes, in the control room."

"Can you use it to address any guests or anyone else still in the building to come to the lobby? We need to get some things in order."

"Yeah, I can do that."

"Good, get them down here. Put those guns in a secure place and I'll be right back. I have an errand to do."

"Bishop, I can't do what you do."

"Austin, you're the man now. Your dad would expect this of you, and you're capable. There's no more time to be a boy. Point and shoot if you have to. I'll be right back."

Bishop left without looking back and climbed past the body he'd dropped, walking down the road going east the way he came. Gusts of wind blew flurries by, metal street signs barely visible above the snow shuddered in the strong breeze. He had no doubt many of the nearly naked boys would die out there tonight.

Fighting the wind, several blocks later Bishop stopped where his snowmobile lay covered and half-hidden in the snow from earlier that morning. Looking for the little boy who'd landed in the icy berm, he only saw boot marks near where the child was thrown. He had no idea if the boy lived or died, but at least he had a chance.

Starting the snowmobile in near darkness, Bishop soon pulled up to the storage unit. With his night vision on, his heart pounded the closer he came. There was no mistaking something had taken place by the marks in the snow and blood splatters on the walls near his unit.

"Maeve?" he yelled. "Maeve?"

Seeing the lock obliterated, he held an AR-15 out and ready, having no idea what he might find on the other side. He slowly lifted the door.

Inside, he found her glowing eyes watching him, and her hands trembled around her Glock that aimed at him.

"Maeve, it's me, Bishop." He lifted off his helmet as she rushed into his arms. His voice alone confirmed his identity.

"Oh thank God, it's you."

He held her tight. She couldn't stop shaking. "It's me, it's going to be OK now."

Taking her in his arms, he realized soon the cold temperatures would be too much. He had to get them to safety now. Having cleared one menace, he now needed to get them somewhere warm.

"Let's go," he said and loaded them onto Jake.

As the snow fell, he found himself retracing his previous tracks back to the hotel. With Maeve and the both children mounted on the back of his horse, he led them down the familiar road. But this time, it was different. In the houses lining the streets, people didn't shy from the windows now. They opened their doors and yelled out to him.

"Hey, mister!"

He waved to them. "Follow me," he said.

By the time he could see the hotel, a bright warming light glowed from within. Streams of dark figures were filing into the building.

Soon they were surrounded by people in dark rags on either side. The crowd of townspeople who'd watched from their silent houses made way for him between them, and then someone began to clap. Another took up the cheer, and Bishop stopped and looked up to Maeve as if to ask, "What's going on?"

"You saved the town, Bishop. You saved us all."

Chapter 46

Bishop stopped near the entrance and helped Maeve and the children down from the horse. As he went inside, the first thing he saw was Austin's smiling face.

Already a banquet table was set up, and warm food was in preparation. People lined the inside of the enormous lobby where the cheery fireplaces blazed.

"Who are these people?" Bishop asked Austin as he gazed at the many workers passing out plates of food and warm blankets.

"Some of them are the guests who were hiding out here. Others are staff who stayed away when Roman took over. I sent out word to get them to come back and help. Word travels fast."

Austin was in his element. He shouted orders to several people. "Someone take this man's horse to the office at the end of the hall and give him whatever he wants."

Bishop laughed and handed the reins to an older gentleman who took Jake away. Then he led Maeve and the children to a seat near the fireplace to get them warm. Austin stopped by and said, "I've got a room for you and your family upstairs."

Before Bishop could correct him, he handed him the keys. Maeve put her hand over his and said, "You're not getting out of my sight again, mister. We can share."

His eyes found hers. He wasn't sure if he could share the same space with anyone for long, but for her, he would try.

They sat down on a cushioned bench. Ben at his right and Maeve, with Louna on her lap, on his left. Their rifles by their sides. People were still filing in with only the rags on their backs covered in snow, looking like the ghosts they nearly were, when suddenly Louna screamed out.

Bishop jumped and held his rifle out. The blond hair of the woman running toward them was an unmistakable match for the girl's.

Maeve cried, "You're alive!" but that was all that was needed to be said. It was clear the woman clutching Louna, both of them sobbing, was a relative. Maeve clung to Bishop's side after giving the girl up freely to her mother.

Bishop took a blanket and wrapped it around them, enclosing them in safety together. There was no separating the two.

Like a scene from a medieval past, people huddled in groups eating from plates handed to them while candle and firelight fought off the darkness from outside.

Austin's helpers passed out hotel room keys to those that had no place to stay, washed dishes, and gave directions, and everyone pitched in where needed.

After they'd eaten, Bishop held a sleeping Ben to his shoulder and led Maeve through the crowds and up the elevator. When the doors were shut, Maeve said, "How did you do this?"

He lifted his shoulder as if he had nothing to say.

"Man of few words."

Chapter 47

With dim light cascading into the room, Bishop woke. At first, he had no idea where he was, but as he stared up at the white ceiling adorned with metal sprinkler heads instead of the cave ceiling of his typical surroundings, the reality of what had taken place a week ago rushed back to him. *Maeve...Ben?*

He launched himself from the couch and found them both lying motionless on the queen bed, still sound asleep. Nearing the side of the bed, Maeve's hair cascaded out over the pillow like a radiating flame. Softly snoring, she had one hand clutched around her son's wrist; even in sleep she was a good mother.

Without resisting the urge, Bishop nudged a strand of hair out of Maeve's face, exposing her slender neck, and then he wished he hadn't because the bruising there in shades of purple and green caused the muscles in his arms to flex with malicious intent against those who had hurt her.

Despite that, Maeve was every bit as beautiful, possibly more so, in her peaceful sleeping state. Tearing his eyes away from her was difficult, but then he heard a distant noise. A familiar noise. When he walked over to the window and looked out over the ice, he recognized the man on the snowmobile from before. There were two of them this time, and they were heavily armed.

Just in case this meant trouble for them, Bishop quickly put on his outerwear and grabbed his recovered AR-15 and Beretta out of habit as he began to leave.

"Where are you going?" Maeve asked sleepily.

He wasn't used to answer to anyone about his actions. He stared at her, and she reached for him, her arm outstretched for him to take.

Staring at her gesture, as if this meant more than mere words, he went to her and wrapped his rough hand beneath her slender forearm. His voice raspy, he whispered, "There's a party of men coming over the ice. I need to go out and meet them—see what they want and where they're from. I saw them once before. He seemed dejected. I need to make sure they're no threat to us."

She held on to him while she rubbed her sleepy eyes with her other hand. As he watched her, she stared up at him, and then he felt a tug as she pulled him toward her. He bent down as she led him to her lips. Pressing her own to his lightly, she kissed him, and he found himself responding before he'd even made the decision. His arm slid behind her neck, his other behind her back. When they finally pulled away, her look of shock mirrored his own. Never had such an encounter sent such a shockwave through him. "I...I won't be long."

She looked confused suddenly. "Please don't. Please come right back."

"I will," he said and cleared the thick feeling in his throat as he left.

In the lobby, his mind wandered over the past few days while they'd stayed in the hotel. Much had been accomplished. Austin was turning out to be a great leader for the town.

Once downstairs, he found Austin peering out the big window to the south.

"What do you think they want?" Bishop asked, causing Austin to turn.

"I'm not sure. I think that's the sheriff who left and went to Rockford Bay when Roman and Frank were taking over."

Bishop thought about that for a moment. "Would you call the man a coward?"

Austin shook his head. "No, I think he just knew he was beaten. I know he took several people with him and tried to warn the rest. I'm sure he feels responsible, but he has a family and another community to protect there as well."

Bishop nodded as the snowmobiles stopped on the edge of the frozen lake. The riders stepped off, removing their helmets and looking at the building with questions on their faces.

"They're expecting Roman's men to come out and meet them. They look confused."

"You're the boss here, Austin. You want to invite them inside? Ask them what they want. I'll cover you."

"I...I'm not sure. I think you'll be better at negotiating with them."

"I'm not the leader here, Austin. You are. This is your show. You've done a great job of rallying this town so far. I'll back you up."

"OK," Austin said, shifting his weight from one leg to the other.

"I'll go with you, but you're the man. I'm just your backup. You can do this."

Austin nodded. "OK," he said, sounding more confident than before.

Neither of them was prepared for the even colder brisk air tightening their lungs the moment they set foot outside. Drifts of snow had piled up in berms as wisps of air swirled out over the flat ice. Once a winter wonderland, the lake now looked formidable. The men waiting were adorned with frozen mustaches despite the helmets they'd worn.

The temperature had dropped even further, so there was no question of remaining outside for long. Instead, Austin, followed by Bishop with his hand on his rifle, stepped outside. When the other men saw them, Austin attempted to speak, but the wind stole his words right away. Instead, he waved for the two men to follow them into the building.

He and Bishop retreated as the two men cautiously joined them. After shaking off the snow, one man extended his hand to Austin.

"Hi, I'm Carl Hanson. I was sheriff here. I think I've met you before. It's my understanding that Roman has taken over here. I'd like to speak with him if I may."

Clearing his throat, Austin said, "There's been a change in management here. Roman is no longer with us."

Bishop watched as the man looked from Austin to himself and back. Bishop detected fear in the man the second he stepped inside. Carl took a deep breath. "Who's in charge now then?"

Austin stood a little taller than before and glanced at Bishop. "I am."

A look of utter relief washed over the man. He looked to his partner, who had so far remained silent, and Bishop could see tears in his eyes too.

"Then, please, Austin, my people are dying. I need your help."

Austin smiled and led them to a sunken sitting area. The fireplaces kept the lobby so warm that the two men began taking off layers of coats, then held their hands out to the blaze, warming them for the first time in weeks, Bishop guessed.

"Who are you?" Carl asked, referring to Bishop.

Austin answered, "This is my associate, Bishop. He helps me keep things in order."

A smile came to Carl's face. He stretched out his hand to shake Bishop's. "I know a military man when I see one."

Bishop only nodded. The other man with Carl introduced himself as Tom Maloney.

Both men looked scared, thin to the point of starvation, and lost. Whatever they were about to say, Bishop knew the subject concerned their last hopes.

Austin tapped a lady passing by who had a young child at her side. "Miss, could you have the kitchen bring some coffee and breakfast for these two gentlemen?"

She stopped and smiled, and when she did, the child caught Bishop's attention. The little boy…he was the one who'd been flung into the snow. He could tell by the blue eyes and the fact that half of his little forehead was black and blue from the encounter. Feeling a sort of relief, Bishop took a deep breath. He hadn't been able to help wondering about the child.

Bishop returned his attention to the men in front of him, and the surprise on their faces for the simple fare Austin had offered concerned him.

"Austin," Carl began. "I've made this trip two times before." He swallowed hard. "My people in Rockford Bay…they're literally starving to death." He held his hands out wide. "We don't have much to offer you, but we were hoping we could work something out."

Resisting the questions coming to his mind, Bishop held back. He didn't want to step into any position that could be handled by another. Austin, in his mind, was the rightful heir of the hotel and the town, and he would back him as long as he did things right.

"How many people do you have?"

Carl swallowed again. "We were at twelve hundred before the freeze; we're now about eight hundred. We've had some fighting. We had to take down looters for killing others for their food." He wiped his forehead. "I've never seen anything like it. Common people...killing one another for a sack of flour. It's the worst of mankind out there."

"We've seen it too. So eight hundred. I'll tell you we've just gotten things under control here, barely. We have a food shortage here as well. We can't spare much, but we'll put together what we can."

Bishop watched as Carl began to speak, but then the sheriff couldn't contain himself and broke down in tears. His companion patted him on the back and said to them, "His wife died yesterday and his daughter is dying too. It's been really hard."

Austin nodded. "I understand," he said and continued to talk while Carl got a hold of himself. "We've had tough times too. Roman basically sponsored town looting, killed many people. Most of the food was brought here to the hotel. Now we're using our kitchens to feed everyone two meals a day. I wanted to give everything back to the people, but it was an impossible task, so I've appointed the staff to make daily meals instead. Those who have nothing to eat can come here. We even have horse-drawn sleds bringing them in from old bus stops."

Carl laughed at the statement.

"We're back in the pioneer days it seems, and we damn well better figure out how to live through this before it's too late. How long is this Maunder Minimum supposed to last anyway?"

Bishop spoke up then, and they weren't going to like his answer. "This can go on for ten or more years. I hate to be the bearer of bad news, but..." He paused and shook his head. "We won't survive here long term. We're in an ice age."

The two men looked at each other, not trusting or wanting to believe the words. "What do you mean?"

"I mean, all the food you can hunt beyond what we have in our possession will not be enough to survive here. We might as well be at the poles. We can fish the lake for what's survived the sudden freeze there, and we can grow hydroponics in some of the buildings. We can also hunt the woods to oblivion and it will still not be enough to sustain us. We cannot live here for long; this is a temporary situation. We need to get our heads around that and soon, because we need to find a way to travel before it's too late."

***

By the time the men left, their snowmobiles were topped off with fuel and attached with trailers filled with food and medical supplies as well as radio units so that they could communicate better with their neighbors.

The people of Rockford Bay promised to share hunts when they were well enough to do so, and to attend meetings to make decisions on the inevitable evacuation Bishop alerted them to.

Again Bishop and Austin watched the men leave through the great windows, more slowly and more burdened by lifesaving supplies than Bishop thought was wise, but he wasn't going to give Austin a hard time about it. Helping the people in Rockford Bay might pay off in future exchanges. At least he hoped so, because they were going to need it.

Chapter 48

Maeve stood gazing out the frosty, sliding glass window, her arms wrapped tightly around herself. With the blue light cascading onto her, highlighting the red in her hair and the crimson shade of her lips, for the first time in a year, she found herself wanting a man's touch other than her deceased husband's. At first, she felt guilty for the urge, a betrayal of sorts to Roger's memory, and shocked at the realization that perhaps she was no longer grieving her dead husband. The sweet memory of Bishop's kiss kept flashing into her mind and began replacing the pain Roger's death left in her heart.

This morning when he touched her hair, she couldn't help but feel the anticipation of this quiet man kissing her again. Now she had hope, a hope for something she'd never allowed herself in the past. A hope that perhaps someday when he was ready, they might become a family.

If only life were normal. But then again, chaos was what brought them together. That, and a promise Bishop made with her husband. Somehow, she thought, Roger had made this possible. If he couldn't be there to protect them, he put in place a man who could, one whom he trusted with his family. So in the end, it was with Roger's blessing, that she let some of her guilt go and made room to live life with a possibility of love in the future, no matter the dire conditions of the world at hand.

Author's Note

I hope you enjoyed *Surrender the Sun*. I know it's odd, but I'm always looking for new ways to end mankind or at least make life quite difficult to survive. It's how I see the future. Whether it be a pandemic, weather phenomena or an asteroid, I tend to view the future as something more to survive. And those are only a few of the *natural* conditions to deal with out of man's control.

As for the Maunder Minimum, it's a real thing. The *mini ice age* described in the book actually took place. Will it really happen again? That remains to be seen. There is evidence that the same lack of sunspot activity will begin in the year 2030 and last about 10-15 years. There is also arguments contrary to the theory. Perhaps, if it does, it will replenish our glaciers.

By saying this, I by no means am trying to debunk climate change. This is an existing phenomena and I believe this is a part of the overall weather explanation of our planet.

To be among the first to learn about new releases, announcements, and special projects, @AuthorARShaw.com. You can also drop me a note from that location.

***Above all, **please leave a review** for *Surrender the Sun* on Amazon. Even a quick word about your experience can be helpful to prospective readers.

About the Author

Born in south Texas, A. R. Shaw served in the United States Air Force Reserves from 1987 through 1991 as a communications radio operator, where she worked at the Military Auxiliary Radio System (MARS Station) at Kelly AFB, Texas.

Her first novel, *The China Pandemic* (2013), hit #1 in Dystopian and Postapocalyptic genres in May 2014. It was hailed as "eerily plausible," and her characters "amazingly detailed." She lives with her family in Eastern Washington but may flee soon to the hills of Idaho.

You can contact A. R. Shaw directly at AR@AuthorARShaw.com or through her website at AuthorARShaw.com.

Printed in Poland
by Amazon Fulfillment
Poland Sp. z o.o., Wrocław